K-POP DEMON DETECTIVES

TOKYO TAKEDOWN

Bluestone Books
www.bluestonebooks.co

ISBN: 978-1-965636-60-2 (paper over board)

Printed in the United States of America
10 9 8 7 6 5 4 3 2

Front cover design by Katie Jennings Campbell
Interior design by Noora Cox
Illustrations by Lidia Fernandez

K-POP DEMON DETECTIVES

TOKYO TAKEDOWN

STACIA DEUTSCH

BLUESTONE BOOKS

交ダンス
衣類の洗濯
ハンバーガー
飲み物
衣類ファッション
レストラン
楽器店
音
コーヒーショップ
お茶

CHAPTER 1

THE DESIGNER'S STUDIO

"If you think your last concert in Seoul made an impression on fans," Ha Jun said as he led Song Yi, Willow, and Iseul down one alleyway and into another, weaving them through the crowded streets of Tokyo, "just wait until you see what I have arranged for your show tomorrow night. ALIBI's fans will never forget this stop on the tour. Epic, I tell you! It's gonna be EPIC!" He turned left, then right, then left again.

"Are you sure you know where you're going, Ha Jun?" Song Yi asked her brother. "Being the manager of a rising K-pop group is a hard job . . . I know the producer hired you for this gig, but are you sure you're cut out for it?"

Song Yi loved spring weather. When Ha Jun told them all to wear "daily looks," she'd picked a pink-faded top and fitted black shorts. Her floral tote bag was just her style: handwoven and from a local craft fair.

"I'm the best manager you have," Ha Jun replied.

"You're the only one," Song Yi replied. "Did you mean to bring us to the quietest alley in all of Japan?" She gestured toward the decades-old, sun-worn, tired brick buildings. While much of Tokyo glowed bright with lights and flashing neon signs, this part of the city was run-down and completely vacant. They hadn't seen another person since the first left turn.

"Never doubt me," Ha Jun told his sister. "I've got it all under control." He finally stopped in front of a plain, unmarked wooden door.

Song Yi tilted her head, surveying the door. There was no knob. No clear way to enter. "We'll see, won't we . . ."

"I like your vintage vibe, Ha Jun," Willow said, while Ha Jun checked his phone to confirm they were at the right address. "It's nice that you're wearing the bomber jacket I found for you!" He'd paired the charcoal coat with a white T-shirt and khaki joggers.

Willow's baggy, rose-colored balloon pants and long belt were also meant to make her look like a normal person on the street. The trendy crop top might have added to the "off duty" look, but her expensive tennis shoes revealed that she'd recently splurged on herself.

"This doesn't look epic to me," Iseul said, squinting from behind her new clear glasses. She wore a teal short skirt and matching sweater set that she'd had in her closet for years—pure vintage. "We're in nowhere-ville, Tokyo. Staring at a door."

Iseul was uncomfortable with gifts and displays of wealth. Sure, she'd wear the styles that Ha Jun arranged and smile for the cameras, but she was happy to give it all back at the end of the photo shoot or concert.

"Ha Jun, I thought you were taking us to some fancy-schmancy costume designer," Iseul said with an expression that said she really hoped he wasn't. "This math doesn't compute. Usually, *fancy* plus *designer* equals a much more beautiful entryway."

"Patience, friends," Ha Jun said, eyes gliding over the door, searching for . . . *something*.

Song Yi noticed a small black dot embedded in the wood at eye level. It was the size and shape of a spider. She pointed it out to Ha Jun. He nodded like he'd already seen it.

"Can we go inside now?" Song Yi asked.

"Why are you all in such a hurry, *noona*?" Ha Jun

asked Song Yi, using the Korean term of affection for his big sister while fishing in his own leather satchel for some papers and a pen. "My master says, 'The slow fish gets eaten last.'"

"Your new martial arts instructor sure has a lot of sayings," Song Yi replied, rolling her eyes at him. "What does that even mean? Who's the slow fish?"

"I'm not sure," Ha Jun admitted with a shrug. "But the master says it'll become clear in time."

"You're ridiculous," Song Yi said with a chuckle.

"Nah, I'm *awesome*," Ha Jun replied. He handed the girls the paperwork.

"What's this?" Song Yi asked, scanning the document. "An NDA?"

"You got it," Ha Jun said, passing out the pens. "Typical non-disclosure agreement. ALIBI uses them all the time for our own protection. These say that you won't tell anyone what you see in here. Anything that happens in this place stays in this place."

"Since we don't know what this place is," Iseul said, adding her signature, "I'm glad to keep it a secret."

"Mysterious," Willow said. "I do love a mystery." She signed her copy of the document and handed it back to Ha Jun.

Song Yi hesitated. Why would someone want to keep this place quiet? What was behind the unadorned door? "Only one way to find out," she muttered, writing her name on the line.

Ha Jun slipped the papers under the doorframe and waited. There was a rustling sound from inside, then his phone dinged with a text.

"We're A-okay," he said with a mischievous grin. "Now check *this* out." Ha Jun leaned in and pressed his eye against that spiderlike door-dot. An instant later, the lock opened with an echoing click.

"What's up with that?!" Iseul exclaimed. She pushed past Ha Jun to inspect the hidden scanner. "Oh wow. An infrared camera takes a high-res image of the retina. The data is converted into a digital code. The code's programmed to open the door! So much wow!" she gushed.

"Come on. Let's go." Ha Jun said with a smile, ushering the girls inside.

Willow and Iseul stepped inside first and took in the stark, undecorated space.

Song Yi cautiously surveyed the room before committing to enter. The cavernous room had a slick, industrial gray cement floor and no furniture. Dim lights made the space unquestionably spooky.

There was something unsettled in the air. Song Yi tucked a strand of her brown, shoulder-length hair behind her ear as a chill ran down her spine.

"Where are we?" Song Yi asked, turning back to her brother, who still held the door open.

"This is going to be the best day of your life!" Ha Jun assured her.

"We'll see," Song Yi said, not yet shrugging off her suspicions.

"Trust me," Ha Jun said, following her inside.

"Know what would make this the best day ever?" Song Yi asked her friends.

"Ginger tea with lemon?" Willow asked.

"Video game marathon?" Iseul suggested.

"I have another idea . . ." Song Yi raised her hands like cat claws and began tiptoeing toward her brother.

"No!" Ha Jun protested. "Song Yi, no! Not today!"

"Hate to waste this big empty arena." Song Yi tossed down her tote bag and, with a mighty pounce, grabbed Ha Jun by the neck, swinging him into a headlock. She playfully rubbed her knuckles against his cropped black hair.

"Song Yi! Knock it off!" He gasped, head trapped, legs flailing. "You'll get our outfits dirty," he choked. "Stick to songwriting! You're a poet, not a fighter."

"I'm both!" She laughed as she set him free. "You act like a big-time manager, but we all know you're just my baby brother pretending to be all grown up." Song Yi danced around Ha Jun, hands raised in a tae kwon do stance. "Show me what this new martial arts master has taught you."

"Ha Jun can't resist a fight," Willow said, stepping back, out of the way.

"And Song Yi doesn't like to lose," Iseul replied, joining Willow safely against the nearest wall.

"Oh, *noona*, I might be younger than you," Ha Jun said, taking a big breath, "but I'm taller and stronger!" With one hand, he grabbed his sister's outstretched arm, twisting it back and upward.

Song Yi dropped her weight, tumbling them both to the floor. They rolled, like a two-headed ball, across the room.

"I think Song Yi will win this time," Willow said. She twirled one of her long dyed-blonde braids. She had pink bows tied around the bottom of the braids to match the pants. No matter what Willow's hair looked like, if she was setting her own fashion, she liked to wear a bow. Or a few bows twisted together.

"Are you guessing? " Iseul asked. "Or is this one of your intuitive predictions? I'd never bet against your intuition."

“It’s a fact. She may like to tease her brother about his new master, but that kid’s martial arts skills are improving,” Willow said.

“He’d better learn fast,” Iseul said. “Song Yi has mad battle skills.” Just then, blazing ceiling lights flicked on, and the rainbow-colored streaks woven through Iseul’s dark hair shimmered. The harsh yellow beams revealed Song Yi sitting on Ha Jun, whom she had flipped over onto his back.

“Surrender?” she asked her brother, too involved in her battle to register the sudden lighting change.

“Nev—” he began, but the word died on his lips as they both looked up into the stern, frowning face of Yumi Kondo, Japan’s most famous fashion designer.

“Children!” Her expression didn’t flinch. Her eyes bore into Ha Jun and Song Yi like lasers. “Stand up,” she demanded in a soft yet commanding voice.

Ha Jun and Song Yi both jumped to their feet.

“Sorry, sorry, sorry.” Ha Jun bowed with each apology, not looking directly at Yumi Kondo.

Yumi Kondo wore a severe bun that pulled back her skin and made her age difficult to determine. She could have been anywhere from twenty to sixty years old.

“Forgive us,” Song Yi said. “I thought this outing might be another one of Ha Jun’s tricks.” She glanced at her brother's embarrassed red face. "He jokes around a lot."

"I, too, have a younger brother," Yumi Kondo said.

The room grew uncomfortably silent. Not one of the K-pop stars dared to speak—or even move.

Ha Jun stayed low in his bow.

After a long beat, Yumi Kondo crooked a finger at Willow and Iseul, wordlessly directing them to come close to her.

"Let me look at you two." She made a circle with her finger. Willow and Iseul obeyed, turning around slowly as if they were puppets on the great designer's string. Her gaze did not leave them.

"You'll do fine," Yumi Kondo said. She snapped her fingers. A young man, college-aged, entered from a side door so tightly enmeshed in the wall that none of them had seen it in the dim lighting. He wore black, as if trying to fade into the background, and his midnight-black dyed hair gave him the appearance of a shadow. He was pushing a silver-wheeled garment rack. The rack had a long bar with three hangers. Whatever was on those hangers was hidden inside zippered garment bags.

Song Yi noted that he'd be an excellent stagehand, moving the set pieces and props without anyone seeing him.

He parked the cart in the center of the room, then slipped a remote control to Yumi Kondo. Song Yi watched the designer take the device and cradle it in her hands before hiding it in the sleeve of her unadorned, floor-length black kimono. She tightened the black belt around the robe's waist.

Song Yi had a funny feeling that Yumi Kondo's confidence was an act. It was hard to know what was really going on inside her head.

"This is Minato Sato, my intern," Yumi said. "He's shy, doesn't talk much." She waved her hand dismissively as if flicking him away. She certainly wasn't going to roll the garment cart out herself. "*I* have designed personalized, one-of-a-kind jackets for tomorrow night's concert. You'll wear sleek black bodysuits underneath them to give them all the attention they deserve. Thanks to me, ALIBI will shine in Japan."

Minato unzipped the first two jackets from their garment bags, then motioned to Willow and Iseul.

Willow's was bright blue with patterned embroidery down the arms. Aquamarine was her fan color . . .

"Oh!" She exclaimed, leaping forward. "There are crystals sewn into the fabric." She ran her hand over the jacket as she examined the stones. "Blue lace agate for truth and communication. Rose quartz for love, and self-love." Her hand stilled. "Lapis lazuli bonds lifelong friendships." Willow's eyes sparkled with joy as she turned to Yumi Kondo. "It's perfect. It feels like you know my heart's deepest desires."

"I do," Yumi Kondo said, nodding.

Minato revealed the second jacket: a silver so pure that it was practically translucent. He showed Iseul the hidden switch that controlled the integrated mini light bulbs sewn into the shiny fabric. He said softly to Iseul, "Yumi Kondo envisioned this for you."

Song Yi noted that Minato said "envisioned" and not "sewed" or "created." She wondered who had actually done the work on the jackets. Was it Minato? Or had someone else hand-stitched the fabric and sewn on the buttons?

"It's my fan color, too: chrome!" Iseul flicked the switch inside her jacket. "And it has LEDs!" she cried as the jacket glittered and glowed. Iseul could control the colors, patterns, speed, and rhythm of the flickering lights. "You know my heart, too!" She bounded forward, arms wide, to hug Yumi Kondo, but the designer quickly stepped back and away.

Iseul played it cool. She dropped her hands and pretended that emotion hadn't gotten the best of her. "I mean, yeah, thanks for the costume."

Finally, Minato carefully unwrapped the third jacket. He took more time and was more careful with this one than the other two.

Song Yi held her breath, waiting for the reveal. If the other jackets had been perfect for her friends . . . what would hers be like?

The first thing she noticed was that the jacket was red. Bright ruby.

That was *her* fan color, which had always seemed strange to Song Yi. In her real life, she tended toward lighter, pale colors—nothing as glittery and flashy as the jacket that Minato held toward her. She wanted her voice and dance moves to command more attention than her costume.

But there was something extra about this jacket that drew her attention.

The ruby sequins winked at her, forming patterns that would be imperceptible to anyone else's eyes, but not Song Yi's.

Nothing ever escaped her. If there had been a loose thread or a sequin out of place, she'd have noticed. Her power of observation was what made her a great leader for their K-pop group. She caught the tiniest mistakes in their choreography. Her mind flashed beats and lyrics together, knowing how to keep them perfectly in sync. If something was off, Song Yi was always the first to discover it. Her attention to detail was also what made her perfect for ALIBI's secret, off-stage life.

Song Yi chided herself for not having noticed the hidden door at the back of the studio where the designer had entered. She should have taken the time to let her eyes adjust to the shadows. She'd allowed her brother to distract her when she should have seen that the room was more than it seemed. She hoped it wasn't a sign that she was losing her edge.

After assuring herself that an error like that wouldn't happen again, Song Yi let Yumi Kondo put the jacket on her.

"Dance and sing in it, but don't sit, okay?" said Yumi Kondo.

"Why?" Song Yi asked, wondering what was behind the warning.

"Because I said." Yumi Kondo smoothed the shoulders and stepped back from Song Yi.

The jacket might have been a little too much for her taste, but Song Yi had to admit it was somehow perfect. Better than perfect: Every sequin, every stitch, worked together in harmony. Song Yi knew there was more to the jacket than shape and style.

She'd seen Minato hand Yumi Kondo a remote control. Her eyes traveled to the tiny black box in Yumi Kondo's hand.

Yumi Kondo saw the shift in Song Yi's attention. Her eyes seemed to . . . smile?

"Do you want to see the jacket's full glory?" the designer asked.

"Yes!" Song Yi said. Her voice betrayed her excitement.

Yumi Kondo pressed a button. A single spotlight dropped from the ceiling. The concentrated beam of light hit the glitter and sequins, transforming the jacket from a beautiful costume into something spectacular.

Song Yi means "one flower," but that hadn't felt special to her until now. When the light hit the jacket, wisps of crimson floated off her back, rising in the air like holographic smoke.

The holograph swirled around Song Yi until she was encased in a giant crimson *mugunghwa*, the national flower of South Korea. Each petal unfolded in a slow rhythm that Song Yi knew would match, beat for beat, their most popular song from the new album: a dance track called "Red Pulse."

"Show me," Yumi Kondo commanded.

The three K-pop stars of ALIBI came together under the spotlight and belted out the tune's first notes before breaking into the viral moves.

And Song Yi was right.

Willow and Iseul's jackets brought flair, but Song Yi's jacket shined magnificently. The holographic flower unfurled in time with the lyrics and the choreography.

When they harmonized the last note, the flower dissipated into Ha Jun's raucous applause. "That's what I'm talking about!" he cried out. "No one will ever forget when ALIBI performed in Tokyo!"

Iseul gushed, "Wow! So much wow."

"That jacket is perfect for you," Willow told Song Yi.

"How'd you do it?" Song Yi asked Yumi Kondo. "How did you know what to create for me? For each of us?"

Yumi Kondo stared at the three K-pop celebrities as if seeing them there for the first time and whispered, "Pure magic."

"Sure is!" Ha Jun said, breaking into the moment of awe. "Wrap the costumes up, Minato. We have a photo shoot in fifteen minutes."

"I want to remind you that the jackets are on loan for the Tokyo concerts only," Yumi Kondo said.

"We understand," Ha Jun replied. "That's our usual arrangement."

Song Yi wondered whether her brother might be able to convince Yumi Kondo to let them take the jackets on the rest of ALIBI's world tour. The fans were going to love them! She'd leave that to Ha Jun to figure out later.

Minato took the jackets from the girls and headed back toward the hidden door, leaving the wheeled garment rack behind. Song Yi heard Iseul gasp as Minato stepped out of view.

"What's wrong?" Song Yi asked.

"Didn't you see it?" Iseul pointed at the doorway.

"See what?" Willow rushed to put an arm around her friend.

"The demon!" She turned to look at Song Yi. "When Minato walked by, I saw a demon moving with him."

"What are you talking about?" Song Yi raised an eyebrow. "A *demon*?"

"Minato held my jacket and Willow's jacket in one hand. In his other hand was your jacket, with a small horned demon peeking out of the sleeve." She wrapped her arms around herself and shivered.

"That's a whole lot of nonsense," Ha Jun assured Iseul. "You obviously just thought you saw something. All three *demon-free* jackets will be delivered to the performance center in the morning." He put a hand on her back. "Maybe you're just hungry. Let's grab some *ramyeon* on the way to the photo shoot." He led the girls out into the alley.

"Hang on!" Song Yi realized she had forgotten her tote bag and hurried back inside to grab it.

As she reached for her bag, Song Yi noticed Yumi Kondo still standing exactly where she'd been when they left.

The designer stood, staring away from Song Yi, not even reacting to her noisy return. Or her call of "Thank you!"

In fact, Yumi Kondo didn't move or respond at all. She stood, face frozen in a combination of admiration and suspicion, like a dark, meditative statue, staring silently toward the hidden studio door.

CHAPTER 2

MISSING

"Show starts in exactly sixty minutes," Ha Jun announced as he stuck his head into the dressing room. "That's three thousand six hundred seconds."

"Duh, dude. We know!" Song Yi, seated in the hairstylist's chair, pointed to a big countdown clock on the wall. A makeup artist brushed bronzer on her cheeks while the hairdresser smoothed stray ends. They moved quickly, in tandem.

"That horologe tells time in analog, digital, and binary!" Iseul said, clearly impressed. She fell back onto a small leather sofa and plopped her lace-up boots on the coffee table. "Best clock ever." She explained the binary feature, and though Song Yi had no clue what she was talking about, she loved seeing her friend so excited to explain it.

It was crucial that the members of ALIBI knew when to get onstage. They'd once been so distracted by a side mission that they had missed their first cue by nearly two hours. The incident had happened in their hometown, Seoul, but ALIBI's dedicated fans had waited patiently for them. Anywhere they went in the world, the fans would wait faithfully. But Ha Jun thought it was rude to make them wait and insisted that they add more visual reminders so they'd never be late again.

Ha Jun also insisted that ALIBI arrive at the stadium at least an hour before start time and stay where he could see them until the show ended.

"The wise warrior arrives before the sun gets bored," Ha Jun said, taking a full step into the dressing room. "That's what my master says."

"That makes zero sense. As usual," Song Yi replied. Her hair and makeup were finished. It was Willow's turn in the transformative chair. Although there were several small chairs around the room, Willow liked to stand before the show, to help stretch and warm up her muscles.

This backstage room had been specially prepared for ALIBI. It was an unremarkable space, a large empty canvas, that could be altered to the taste of the performers. ALIBI liked to be together when they prepped. There was a couch, a coffee table, the simple stylist area with a swivel chair and mirror, and a small bathroom where they'd get dressed and undressed, and could shower if they wanted after the show.

Ha Jun, based on his martial arts instructor's advice, insisted that the room be kept clean and simple. Only the most basic elements were provided so they could get ready.

The governor of Tokyo had sent the group traditional kimonos to welcome them to Japan. The robes were hanging on the back of the bathroom door. They each matched the girls' new jackets in color and tone.

The girls were secretly hoping that they'd be able to keep their amazing jackets for their next show in Athens, Greece. Designer gifts were usually returned at the end of the visit, but you never knew what Ha Jun might make happen. He liked to keep a few of his plans, like the visit to the fashion designer's studio, under wraps.

Song Yi handed out the kimonos, threw hers on over her street wear, and admired it in a long mirror. "The only phrase I've liked from the master, so far, is, 'Knowing comes when knowing needs.'"

"Hmmm," Willow said. "Confusing and profound, all at the same time."

"Master Cho is a genius," Ha Jun said with a satisfied nod.

Willow's blonde braids were smoothed, then woven with garden flowers and auspicious crystal beads. Iseul preferred to have her hair long and wavy at concerts, and to let her multicolored streaks reveal themselves.

"Not too much gel this time," Iseul told the stylist in a shy voice. "I mean, unless you think I need it."

Song Yi sighed. Iseul struggled with asking for what she wanted. They all did, but Iseul had the hardest time.

None of the girls had come from great wealth. Iseul's family worked on a goat farm in a small town several hours outside of Seoul. Willow's parents, one American-born and one Korean, owned a bookstore that specialized in mystery novels. Song Yi and Ha Jun were raised by their grandparents after their parents disappeared eight years earlier, when Song Yi was ten and Ha Jun was eight. Their grandparents owned a flower shop, and they lived next door to it, in a modest row-style apartment.

The threesome had been hand-selected and recruited. They'd each received a mysterious letter in the mail from a mysterious music producer, welcoming them to a brand-new K-pop group called ALIBI and providing directions to their training location. After that, they hadn't heard from him again, and they'd never met him in real life. When

Song Yi got her letter, Ha Jun got a different one. Even though he was young and inexperienced, he'd been offered the job of manager. Once he said yes, and the girls were all on board, Ha Jun began getting texts and emails. He was the only one who ever communicated with the producer.

After just a few months of training, ALIBI headed out to perform local shows across Korea. Still, none of them knew the producer's name, but as promised, money flowed in and bills were paid. The local shows were popular, their status grew, and now here they were a year later, at the second stop on a world tour!

The producer coordinated the shows—*and* their mystery-solving side gigs.

Keeping secrets from the public was difficult when fans seemed to know everything about ALIBI. But there was one thing the fans couldn't know: Behind the music, dance, publicity, fashion, and sold-out shows, ALIBI was a force in solving supernatural mysteries.

When signs indicated that a demon was near, ALIBI was on the case—to identify the demon, capture it, and then safely dispatch it to the producer. Sometimes the group stumbled into a mystery on their own; other times, the producer assigned them a mission. Either way, there were *always* plenty of exciting side gigs. They'd been tracking demons and solving demon-related mysteries since their first group rehearsal.

The girls never needed the producer's help. They had natural skills, handmade weaponry, and determination. They hadn't lost a demon yet! Their detective work, on top of keeping the K-pop fans happy, made for very full and busy days.

Once their hair and makeup were finished, they thanked their stylists and watched them leave.

"We're at the point of no distractions," Ha Jun said as he pointed at the clock. "It's 5:30 post meridian, or 17:30 on a twenty-four-hour schedule . . ."

"Binary time: hour one-zero-zero-zero-one, minute one-one-one-one-zero," Iseul said with a laugh. Goat farmers had a lot of free time, and Iseul used that time to learn other things: computer coding, how to play an orchestra of instruments, multiple languages, carpentry, sewing, and the list went on. There were hundreds of things Iseul knew how to do that most people don't.

Song Yi put her hands on her hips. "Well, dear brother, if you want us to be ready, where are the jackets?"

"Thought you'd never ask!" He opened the door to the hallway and whistled in three short bursts. No one came. "Minato!" Still no one. "Minato?" Silence. Ha Jun turned to the girls, "I'll be right back."

He rushed out the door, into the hallway.

"We're going after him, aren't we?" Iseul asked Song Yi.

"Of course." Song Yi looked at Willow and Iseul with a raised eyebrow.

"Whatcha do-do-do!" the girls sang out simultaneously, and then, imitating a dance move from their hit song, "Wild Wild," the girls whipped off their kimonos, tossed them aside, and revealed their . . . off-duty clothes. If they had to go out this way, they hoped the audience would think their casual look was cool.

"This is how every mystery starts, isn't it?" Willow remarked. "Something weird happens, like something goes missing." She raised her palms for a group high five and said the group's mantra: "Reveal. The. Truth."

Iseul held back. A wee bit of fear always kept her focused and grounded. She grabbed her tablet off the coffee table and opened a blank Notes page. "Okay. Now, I'm ready." She gave Willow's palm a reluctant light slap.

"Come on, ALIBI!" Willow embraced any opportunity for adventure.

"Whoa. Slow your roll," Song Yi told them. "The producer didn't alert us to anything suspicious in Japan. And as far as we know, nothing is wrong—yet."

"Uh, our costumes are missing," Willow said.

"Might be a coincidence?" Song Yi suggested, and yet they all knew Song Yi didn't believe in coincidences.

"Sure . . . and yet . . ." Willow dug in, "Iseul saw a horned demon on *your* jacket."

Song Yi pinched her lips, then said to Iseul, "Yeah. You should probably write that down." She shrugged and gave a small smile. "Just in case something is going sideways."

"Already done," Iseul said, turning the tablet to face Song Yi.

They headed into the hallway.

Ha Jun was coming toward them, having failed to find Minato, Yumi Kondo, or their jackets.

"Where were the jackets supposed to be?" Willow asked Ha Jun.

"Minato said he'd personally deliver them at 5:30. On the dot. He promised." Ha Jun began to move down the hall. The girls followed.

"Minato?" Ha Jun opened every door they passed, sticking his head into storage closets and other dressing rooms. "Yumi Kondo said she'd arrive at 5:50 to do one last check and walk you to the stage. She wanted to see the costume reveal."

"Minato is late, and Yumi Kondo hasn't arrived," Song Yi said, considering. She began peering into the doors that Ha Jun had already checked.

"No jackets," he said. "I looked in those."

"Maybe I'll see something you missed."

"Show-off," he said with a sigh.

"Hey, everyone—over here," Iseul called out. She was standing by a tech display panel, a tech assistant by her side. "While you were door-checking, I asked Akiko to review the footage from the hallway just outside the dressing room door."

Akiko, a seasoned tech assistant for the concert venue, had rewound the security footage and was pointing silently at the screen. His close-cut gray hair and wrinkled brow reflected all the years he'd been working in technology.

"That's Minato," Iseul said, pushing up her glasses as she pointed at the image of the design intern they'd met earlier. He was seen on screen wheeling the same rack from the studio, with three garment bags hanging, toward their dressing room. "At exactly one-zero-zero-zero-one, timestamp one-one-one-one-zero." She looked at the others. "Aka 5:30. The security feed spikes, then fades to white. It's still offline."

"Sorry that I didn't catch the drop-out," Akiko said, blowing a light powdering of dust off the computer keyboard. "I stepped away for a second." His fingers flew over the keyboard. "Scrubbing back to the micro-glitch."

"Are you using a jog wheel?" Iseul asked. "That's so old school!"

"Old school works!" Akiko said, running a hand over his stubbled chin. "Rerouting . . . okay. Timecode synced." A few more keystrokes. "And there—the feed's back online."

Akiko played the video again in slow motion, zooming in for closer views. When Iseul was satisfied, the group thanked Akiko and walked away to discuss.

"It doesn't look like Minato ever went inside the dressing room!" Willow said. "But we can't be sure."

"If there wasn't an electrical outage, or a programming error, there might be a demon involved," Iseul said.

"There's for sure a demon at work here," Willow agreed.

"We need facts. I haven't seen the demon with my own eyes yet," Song Yi pointed out. She turned to Iseul. "But can you write down what happened in the security video?"

"Just in case there's a demon?" Willow asked with a chuckle.

"Or a thief," Song Yi said, then added with a wink, "or a demon."

Ha Jun broke into the conversation: "This might be dangerous. Maybe you should all stay here with Akiko, and I'll go back to the room." He raised his hands in a karate stance. "If a demon knocked out the video, I'll take it down."

"Not if I take it down first!" Song Yi shoved past Ha Jun and started running back toward the dressing room, where it all began. Willow and Iseul were hot on her heels, leaving Ha Jun behind.

"No fair! Wait for me!" he shouted, rushing to catch up.

By the time he reached the dressing room, ALIBI was already there—staring at the garment rack that now stood near the couch.

"Wait," Willow said. "I see only two garment bags." She reached for the closest one and opened it. The bright blue shine and stitched-in crystals winked at her. "My jacket's here." She ran her hand over it. "Looks perfect to me."

Iseul opened the second garment bag. Silver sparkled and shined under the fluorescent room lights, and though the LEDs were turned off, Iseul could see that the wiring was pristine. "Mine's ready for the show," she said.

Both Iseul and Willow then turned to Song Yi.

"It's my jacket that's missing." At this point, she'd been looking forward to the blooming flower effect it had and was ready to step out of her comfort zone in that flashy ruby red. The jacket reveal would have been a monumental moment in their performance. But there wasn't enough time to wallow in disappointment. The clock on the wall clicked forward to 5:50.

"We can't wear our jackets without Song Yi's," Willow said. Iseul agreed.

Song Yi turned to her brother. "What do you want to do, Manager?"

"You only call me that when it's time for hard decisions," Ha Jun snorted. "I don't like this situation. We're cutting it too close and we don't own Yumi Kondo's costumes." He reached for his phone, began to dial, then stopped. "I'll call the producer after the show." He tucked his phone back into his pocket. "I thought we wouldn't need the Seoul costumes in Tokyo, but it turns out I was wrong. They're packed in a box . . . somewhere . . . I'll go find them."

"What did you say?!" Yumi Kondo flung open the dressing room door and sauntered into the room. Ha Jun froze. "You girls will not wear the costumes from . . ." she coughed dramatically "*Seoul*."

"They were also made by a top designer," Ha Jun pointed out.

"Nonsense. That designer is the worst." She made an expression of utter disgust. "My jackets were specially designed to set the *look* for ALIBI in Japan. Why would you even *suggest* something else?"

Song Yi pointed at the garment rack. "Minato is missing, and so is my jacket."

"The ruby jacket is missing?" Yumi Kondo gasped. "Who is trying to sabotage *my* moment?"

"Uh, Minato is missing too," Iseul said.

Yumi Kondo brushed that off. "He's so quiet, he's probably around here somewhere and you just can't see him." She nodded approvingly. "I trained him to stay in the background as he should."

"He's not here . . ." Willow swished her hand around the room.

“He’ll be fired for incompetence.” Yumi Kondo began moving hangers back and forth between Iseul and Willow’s jackets, as if the red one was hiding between them and they’d all overlooked it. Finally, after the clock ticked another minute closer to the concert, she said, “It really is gone.” She sank onto the couch with a whoosh of her kimono.

Song Yi noticed the kimono was the same one she’d worn in the studio. Ha Jun and ALIBI often wore the same clothing for different public appearances. That was normal. But for Yumi Kondo, a great designer, Song Yi thought she’d want to show off her designs.

When Yumi Kondo had whooshed onto the couch, Song Yi also had seen a cloud of dust rise into the air. She’d seen Iseul whoosh onto that same sofa and hadn’t noticed the dust.

“Dust!” Yumi Kondo gasped, staring at the shimmer that fell around her.

“Can you please stand back up?” Song Yi asked her.

The designer leapt up, staring at the sofa.

Song Yi leaned her face close to the couch. She raised the pillow. Then she peered underneath the sofa. When she stood up again, she was holding a single red sequin in her hand.

"Is that from your jacket?" Iseul asked, leaning in to look.

"I think so," Song Yi said. She needed to save it to study it later, but her shorts didn't have a pocket. She grabbed her red kimono and placed the small red glittering dot in the narrow sleeve pocket.

Willow traced a finger through the dust on the floor. It shimmered and glistened like crushed mica or tiny bits of opal. "What is this stuff?"

Iseul swiped up some dust. "Is this photonic silk residue?" She looked at Yumi Kondo. "I've heard of it, but never seen it used."

"Of course it is," Yumi Kondo said. She stared hard at Iseul's glowing finger. "Photonic silk is the perfect holographic reflector for the flower effect."

"Oh wow!" Iseul said, eyes wide. "You've created a nano-filament that is environmentally safe!"

A look flashed between them as they realized they shared a common respect for science and its creative applications.

"The jacket wouldn't release the silk material unless something rubbed against it," Yumi Kondo said. She looked at Song Yi. "That's why I told you not to sit. It was tightly sealed—once the seal is broken, the jacket would continue to leave this residue behind." She rubbed her chin. "But wait. I believe I can fix that problem if I use a different compound . . ." Lost in thought, Yumi Kondo began pacing.

"We all know I didn't sit or stand or sleep in the jacket. I never even had it at the theater." Song Yi squinted at the dressing room floor. Wood planks covered it end to end. She got down on her knees to scan for more dust.

"Stop!" Ha Jun reprimanded. "Do not mess up your hair and makeup! We pay a lot for you to look better than usual."

Song Yi rolled her eyes at her brother. "Better than usual? Is that a compliment?"

"Just don't get dirty." He nudged her aside. "I'll look."

Crawling like a baby, Ha Jun scooted across the floor, following the trail of photonic dust. It led them all out into the hallway and to an obvious panel in the floor: a large square with a handle that was almost perfectly flush with the floorboards.

Ha Jun pried the panel open and peered down. There, under the floorboards, was a dark pit of a storage space. They saw a stack of boxes marked “lights” and . . . hiding between the boxes, the missing intern!

Minato was curled up in a ball and shivering. They could hear him muttering to himself over and over again, “Fame brings fortune.”

CHAPTER 3

DEMON

With just seven minutes before showtime, Song Yi gathered her friends, her brother, Yumi Kondo, and Minato back inside the dressing room.

They had to be cautious. Solving demon-linked mysteries was ALIBI's side job, but it had to remain a secret for the safety of the public. Imagine the chaos if everyone knew there were demons lurking, and they tried to find them and vanquish them themselves. It was a job best left to experts.

When ALIBI was in Seoul, a demon had invaded a clock shop and tried to manipulate time. The girls had figured out that everyone was either late or early, and they'd hunted the creature down. Then there was the time when a hungry demon thought noodles would bring her ultimate power.

This jacket mystery was different, though. It was the first time they were personally affected by a mysterious event.

There was a good chance that the jacket's disappearance had something to do with whatever it was that Iseul saw in its sleeve earlier that afternoon. But until a demon's existence was logically proven, they also had to consider that a human might be responsible for the missing jacket.

And now, tick tock, they only had six minutes before showtime.

Minato leaned back, sinking into the couch cushion. Song Yi sat next to him on one side, Willow on the other. Iseul, taking notes, sat on the floor facing them while Yumi Kondo paced.

Ha Jun took management very seriously, and, with time ticking away, had hurried off in search of the costumes ALIBI had worn in Seoul.

"Where is the jacket?" Yumi Kondo stopped pacing and turned to glare at Minato. He stared back blankly. "What. Did. You. Do?" She pronounced each word slowly as if he might not understand her meaning.

"Can we talk alone?" Minato whispered to Song Yi. He tilted his head at Yumi Kondo and lowered his voice even more. "She oozes bad chi."

"Yumi Kondo, can you please go out and search for the jacket?" Song Yi asked. "Your genius and expertise might lead you to it before the show."

"I'd rather—" Yumi Kondo began.

“Please,” Iseul added her voice. “I want to wear my beautiful jacket, but I won’t unless Song Yi has hers.”

“Me too,” Willow said. “Please go help Ha Jun. Maybe we won’t need the Seoul costumes.”

“Ha Jun needs me,” the designer said at last. She pulled the remote control from her black kimono sleeve. “Perhaps I can make the red jacket holograph flash?”

“Thank you,” Song Yi said, rising to bow.

The instant Yumi Kondo was out of the room, Minato the Silent became Minato the Chatty.

“Oh, she makes me so jumpy, that one. She stares at me with those dark pools for eyes, never blinks. And the constant frown—did you notice the frown?” He didn’t wait for any of the girls to reply. “She’s scary.”

“What—” Song Yi began, but Minato jumped right back in.

“I brought the jackets to your dressing room. I promise I did. Just like the evil boss demanded.” He sought eye contact with Song Yi and added, “I need this job. Very badly.” She nodded, knowing he’d continue. “I was outside the door at 5:30, just like I’d promised, when the demon appeared.”

“Demon?” Willow asked.

"What did it look like?" Iseul asked. She both did and didn't want to know.

"Wee. Like a mouse."

Iseul and Willow exchanged a glance. Song Yi stayed focused on Minato.

"With horns gently shaped upward. And glowing golden eyes."

Iseul began writing down the description in her notes. "I didn't see the eyes," she told Song Yi.

"Did you see it?" Minato asked, quickly turning to her.

"I—" Iseul began. "I don't know. Tell us when you last saw all three costumes." She wanted to encourage Minato to talk more quickly. The show was set to begin in just a few minutes.

"I wheeled the garment rack to the door, like I said." He pointed toward the hallway. "I raised my hand to knock." He imitated the motion. "And then I saw the demon!" He dropped his hand. "The creature ran down the hallway, and I . . . well, I couldn't leave the expensive jackets in the hall to chase the demon, so I took the cart with me and chased it around the corner."

"That must have been when we came out," Willow said. "We didn't see you or the jackets."

"I lost the demon, so I came right back to the dressing room. I put the cart, with all three jackets, right here." Minato stood and crossed to the spot in front of the couch where the wheeling cart still stood.

"The demon popped its head out of your"—he pointed at Song Yi "—garment bag. And hissed at me." He tried to imitate the sound and the face the demon had made.

Willow couldn't help it: She laughed.

"It was terrifying," he assured Willow. "I ran away."

"And hid yourself in the storage space?" Song Yi asked.

"Yes," he said. "I'd have stayed there all night if you hadn't come. I wasn't going to come out and risk seeing the demon again." Minato lowered his eyes to the floor. "I'm ashamed that I am a coward."

"I see . . ." Song Yi said. The clock ticked another minute closer to the concert. "I only have one question, Minato."

He raised his head. "Yes?"

"When did you put on my jacket and take the selfies?"

"I . . . what?" he gasped.

Willow and Iseul looked at each other in shock.

"Well, there are some holes in your story. First, you were brave enough to chase the demon with the costumes, but then so scared you hid in a hole."

"It turned and hissed at me!" Minato said. "That's when I hid in the hole."

"I can accept that," Song Yi said. "But what I can't accept is that there is fine shimmering dust all over the couch. I believe you sat down right there wearing my jacket." She narrowed her eyes.

"Me?" Minato sputtered in protest.

Song Yi held out the single sequin toward him. "I found this under the couch." She wiped her hand across the couch, picking up shimmering dust. "And this dust was left behind when someone leaned back against the couch wearing the jacket."

"Why would I wear your costume?" Minato said, defensively. "I know the rules."

"You tell me," Song Yi said. "Why, Minato?"

Minato was silent for the first time since Yumi Kondo left the room. He refused to look any of them in the eyes.

"We have to go do the show!" Iseul said after looking at the clock. "Minato, answer the question: Did you take a selfie wearing Song Yi's jacket?"

"Yes," he softly admitted at last. "I'm again ashamed. A fan emailed me. He said that he's your biggest fan and offered me money to send him a photo of the costumes before the show. I thought . . ." he sighed.

"I thought it would be the most fun to take one of myself in the jacket." He added, "And I need the money."

"You wore my jacket. Sat on the couch. And took the photo," Song Yi said.

"Yes. That's all true. But the demon is real too!" Minato insisted. "Please believe me. As soon as I sent the selfie, the demon appeared, swinging from the garment rack. It hissed at me. I stripped off the jacket, ran away, and ducked safely into the storage space." He pressed his hands together. "I left the jacket here, in the room, and haven't seen it since."

"The sequin probably fell off when you took off the jacket and dropped it on the floor," Song Yi suggested. "You are supposed to be careful with it."

Minato rubbed his watery eyes. "I know. I know."

"Why were you muttering 'Fame brings fortune' when we found you?" Willow asked him.

"The demon kept saying it. And I didn't want to forget." He sniffled and raised his head. "Thanks for reminding me." His voice dropped to a whisper and he turned to Song Yi. "I want to tell you something. When I wore that jacket, I thought I could replace you. I need to earn more money, and the jacket showed me how. It let me imagine a life with great riches. All I had to do was to pretend I was you, a member of ALIBI."

"You think all K-pop stars are rich?" Iseul asked. "A lot of what we have is borrowed, rented, gifted, or sponsored. And when we do make some money, we have to be very cautious with it because fame isn't something you can count on forever."

"I know! But the jacket tried to convince me that I could be a billionaire!" He sighed. "Someone should have told the demon that I am too chicken to go on stage. I can't even speak up to Yumi Kondo." Minato closed his eyes tightly as the memory slipped away. "When I took off the jacket, the feeling was gone."

"Weird," said Willow. "The jacket triggered an illusion."

Iseul wrote down "Fame brings fortune," just as Ha Jun and Yumi Kondo barreled into the room.

"It's time," Ha Jun said. "We need to go—now!"

"Ha Jun and I, we didn't find the red jacket." Yumi Kondo frowned. "It's gone." She shot a piercing glare at Minato.

He winced and bowed low to his boss.

"We *will* find it," Song Yi assured the designer. "But not tonight."

"There are four more shows in Tokyo," Willow said.

"Plenty of time to solve this mystery." Iseul winked.

Song Yi leaned in toward her friends and whispered, "And catch the demon."

"You admit it exists?" Willow asked. "I thought you wanted to see it with your own eyes."

"I still want proof." She shrugged. "I'm just saying that it's possible a demon is involved . . ."

"ALIBI!" Ha Jun broke in. "No more chitter-chattering! Forget the black bodysuits—they don't work without the jackets. You will wear your off-duty look." He tossed the governor's gift kimonos at the girls. "Put these over your street clothes and shake them off when you do that spinny thing during 'Bright City Lights.' Everyone will think it was planned." He pointed at the door. "You have ten seconds to get in place. Now, RUN!"

Song Yi dropped the sequin into the pocket of her kimono as they all rushed off to get ready.

CHAPTER 4

THE TOKYO SHOW

The show was sold out. The Nippon Budokan was packed with no less than 14,471 people. Ha Jun loved this arena mostly because of its name, which literally meant "Martial Arts Hall."

"The name is the game," he said as the girls crowded onto a lift below the stage. In five seconds, he'd press the button and they'd rise, hit the first dance beat, and perform. There'd be no stopping for two hours and forty-seven minutes. The biggest groups did three-plus hours of performance. ALIBI would need more songs to hit that goal, but they were close. The group was always writing new songs, at least when they weren't busy solving mysteries, posing for publicity photos, building up their social media accounts, going to costume fittings, or rehearsing.

"'The name is the game'?" Willow repeated with a smirk. "Is that a quote from your martial arts master?"

"Ha! No. It's wisdom from your manager." He grinned. "I told you how this venue was built for the Tokyo Olympics judo games, right?"

"In 1964," the girls all said together.

"And later housed karate and judo competitions in 2020 . . . blah blah." Song Yi reached out and ruffled her brother's hair.

"I wish you wouldn't do that," he said, pressing his hair back into place.

"It's for good luck!" she said as the lift began to rise. "Bye now!"

"Do well and come back," Ha Jun called out, just like he did before every show. It was his version of "break a leg."

Willow looked at Iseul. "Does he always think there's a chance we won't come back?" They both laughed.

Song Yi didn't laugh along with them. The instant the lift began to rise, she turned her focus inward. The first song was "Wild Wild." She'd written the lyrics just after the producer tapped her to join the group. Song Yi had always written poetry and lyrics, but they'd only been for herself. Once she joined ALIBI, she was able to write songs she could share with the world. With Iseul's amazing ability to play nearly any instrument and Willow's choreography, Song Yi found it easy to bring her music to life.

The lights in the arena were dark. The crowd was hushed.

Song Yi raised her hands, the cue for the spotlights, and said, "We've got this." Three spotlights burst on, and the music immediately started. ALIBI didn't begin like some of the other groups did, with a video intro. They used that for a breathing and water break after the first three songs.

"Wild, wild, wild child . . ." Song Yi belted out, stepping off the lift and heading down the extended runway over the audience.

She didn't have to look to know that Willow and Iseul were directly behind her. The first dance moves called for them to be in a row, peeking out around one another while taking side-by-side sliding steps in their floor-length kimonos.

The crowd screamed their names. They cheered so loudly that the temporary platform shook.

The group often practiced on a trampoline to prepare for the vibration of the stage when the audience roared. For a K-pop performer, balance was clutch.

"Do what you can, divert from the plan . . ." Willow sang while the three performed synced body rolls.

Iseul stepped to the front. "ALIBI says there are many ways to show strength!"

The song ended a few minutes later with a finger heart pop.

There wasn't time to enjoy the audience's applause. ALIBI moved quickly into the next song: "Confetti Heartbeat." This tune was heavy with synthesizer and required a lot of dancing, but not as much singing. This gave them a few opportunities to discuss the mystery.

"So we're looking for a mini demon, like a mouse or a hamster," Iseul said, crossing in front of Willow.

Song Yi spun in a ripple turn, then the others followed in half-beats.

"Remember when a fan gave you a gerbil in Jeju, Song Yi?" Willow said, finishing the rotation.

Song Yi didn't reply. Where dancing came easily to the others, she found that she'd fall off beat if she didn't stay focused. She did, however, manage a nod.

Willow, with her dance steps in perfect time, muttered, "It escaped at our next show, and when we found it in a hatbox, you gave it to Iseul's sister on the farm."

"Soo-ah adores Mimi." Iseul stamped her left foot to the beat drop.

"Wait a second, three, four," Song Yi said. Cross-step switch beat. "Glowing eyes. Three. Four," she continued. "One. Two. Curving horns." Sync drop. "Fame. Fortune. Three. Four."

"Sounds. Like. Three. Four." Willow said, counting the pulses for Song Yi. "Oni! A Japanese demon ogre. I've read about them in the folklore section of my parents' bookstore."

"Are. You. Sure? Four," Iseul asked, rotating on the fourth beat cue.

"I think Willow is right!" Song Yi said. She knew a little about oni from the stories her grandmother had told her. One type of oni starts off small and adorable like a pet animal, but it becomes bigger and more dangerous the more attention it receives. These troublesome horned demons loved to hang out in fashion studios, concert venues, backstage dressing rooms, and rehearsal studios—anywhere that they could latch on to someone who might have fans.

The song ended and the audience shouted with joy.

"If it's the kind of oni my grandmother told me about," Song Yi said, sliding into place, "it could be the size of a cow by tomorrow! Especially with all this applause feeding it and making it grow bigger!"

ALIBI's playlist wasn't a secret, so everyone knew "Bright City Lights" was up next. Their cheers rocked the arena.

"I bet the judo fighters never got this kind of attention!" Willow chuckled as they moved into their new formation: a triangle.

"If you're both right about this, we're gonna want to ask the audience to whisper their exuberance," Iseul said. "A mouse demon would be so much easier to capture than a cow-size one."

"A cow moves more slowly, though," Willow pointed out.

The fans screamed the first lyrics to the song before it even started. "Bags packed, ticket booked . . . bright city!"

"If they keep this up, the demon will be the size of two cows," Iseul said.

"We can still stop it," Song Yi assured them. Spotlights swept the arena and fans raised their light sticks. Some were red, some silver, some blue. Others were the group's unity color: pearl.

Iseul laughed when a few fans waved neon green light sticks. Bringing other K-pop groups' light sticks to a show was a fun thing for social media.

"We won't let the oni grow using our songs, our fans," Song Yi said. She hadn't seen the demon yet herself, but the evidence lined up with what she'd heard about it. "It seems to me that this particular oni is planning to use me and my jacket to get attention and grow. We won't let that happen."

The beat dropped. ALIBI took their places, ready to begin "Bright City Lights."

"Let's get my jacket back," Song Yi said firmly. "Demon free."

"Bright City Lights" had what fans called a "killing part" that was unforgettable. It was a "killer" dance sequence they'd share in their edits and use to create social media challenges. The killing part was the same part that Ha Jun referred to as the "spinny thing."

Today's spin would include the quick change.

As they stepped into a perfectly matched inward rotation, the girls all spun out of their kimonos, letting them fall away. Their normal, everyday street clothes were underneath.

If anyone recognized the outfits as casual, or what they wore to avoid attention, they didn't seem to mind. In fact, the shouting and cheering grew louder than usual.

“What’s bigger than two cows?” Willow asked Song Yi as they entered the dance break. “If that demon gets all this energy, it’s gonna take over the world.”

“I think that’s the idea,” Song Yi said, heel-click jumping with the others before the dramatic, and silly, hair flip arc.

The song ended. The audience was on fire. It was time for a short break backstage. There was a video of the girls’ childhoods before they joined ALIBI.

While the audience laughed at Iseul’s antics on the goat farm, stagehands gathered the kimonos off the stage and laid out three umbrellas for the next song.

One of the stagehands was near Song Yi when she realized something important.

“Hey!” she called to him. “Can you toss me my kimono?”

Instead, the man crossed to her in the wings and handed her the red robe with a bow.

Song Yi returned the bow. She folded the kimono over her arm and reached into the sleeve fold. “I know I hid that sequin here . . .” Just as she felt it, she let out a scream. It echoed through the arena like a wave, bringing the audience to a soft, curious hum. She dropped the sequin back into her pocket and opened her hand to show her friends. There were burn marks where the sequin had touched her fingers.

Ha Jun came rushing forward. "What happened?" he asked in alarm. "The press, the fans, everyone wants to know who got hurt and how." He gave his sister a questioning look. "It was obviously your voice. I can try to convince them it was me, but they won't buy it. What's the matter?"

She showed him her burned hand. "The red sequin."

"Don't move," Ha Jun told her. He darted away and came back with gauze and some cream.

"I'll do the wrap," Willow said, taking the cream and frowning at the label. "Arnica would be better and more natural than this stuff."

"First aid kits don't come with flower extract," Ha Jun said.

"Ice?" Willow said. "Burns need ice."

"Not in the first aid kit." He pointed at the gauze. "No time."

Willow sighed and began to wrap Song Yi's thumb and pointer finger.

"I can't wear this on stage!" Song Yi protested.

"Everyone heard you scream in pain," Iseul said. "We can explain it, and your fans will have compassion."

"No," Song Yi said. "If we mention the sequin or the burn from it, the demon will know we are on the case." She unwrapped Willow's dressing. "I can handle the pain until the show ends."

"Do we put out a message about your very loud scream?" Iseul asked. "I can work something into the light board and run a message if you don't want to talk about it."

"We ignore it and move on, okay?" Song Yi said.

The video they'd played earlier in the show had already told the visual story of Song Yi and Ha Jun's parents' disappearance, giving the audience some background as to why Song Yi was such a sensitive songwriter.

New footage highlighting Willow's amazing tumbling skills was playing when Ha Jun's phone dinged.

"It's the producer," he reported. His eyes scanned the text. "He knows about the oni."

"How?!" Willow exclaimed. "There's no way!"

Iseul looked above them for cameras. "Is it possible he has a live video feed?"

"Doesn't matter how," Ha Jun said as the text dinged again. "He just knows. He's got a message for ALIBI." Ha Jun turned the phone so the girls could see the message as he read it. "You must get the oni before the final show in Tokyo."

Song Yi raised her eyes, as if there were a camera above them, and shouted, "Tell us something we don't already know."

The video of the girls continued with scenes from the Seoul show. They only had a few minutes left before they had to get back on stage.

Ha Jun's phone dinged again.

It was a link to a collection of fan posts from the show.

Dancing fans. Happy fans. Cheering fans.

Ha Jun thumbed through them, sweeping right. Then, suddenly, he stopped.

"You asked for someone to tell you something you didn't know. Well, here it is." He stared at his sister.

ALIBI huddled around Ha Jun to look at the screen.

In one photo, there was a young man, dark hair, smooth skin, his shirt collar pulled up to hide his face.

Song Yi gasped.

He was wearing her red jacket.

"The fan might not know that's my jacket," she said with a tight voice. "Yumi Kondo still has the remote control, so he can't know what that jacket does."

"Is that this arena?" Iseul asked. She peered out from behind the stage to scan the audience. There were too many people, and a lot of them were wearing sequins. "We'll never find him."

"And the remote would never work this far away," she added. "Even if we had it, between the range and the obstructions, the hologram wouldn't expand."

"The demon will lead the way," Willow told them.

"Is that one of the master's quotes?" Song Yi asked.

Willow didn't laugh. She simply pointed to the photo.

It took a minute for them to look beyond the jacket to the glowing eyes and hooked horns of the little oni in the image. It was perched on the jacketed fan's shoulder, partially blocked by the hand of another fan and her raised cellphone.

"That's definitely not a gerbil!" Iseul's jaw dropped. "It's more like a hedgehog with horns!"

"Hedgehogs make wonderful pets," Willow said. "Although the horned demon thing is probably a drawback."

"This is all the proof I need to believe that there's a demon in our midst," Song Yi said. She stared at the photo until the instant they had to go back on stage.

"I'll see if we can ID the fan, or where he's sitting," Ha Jun said, rushing off.

When ALIBI was back on the stage, under the cloak of darkness, waiting for the lights to come on, Song Yi said to the others, "Now the question is: Who took my jacket? Was it the demon or the fan?"

CHAPTER 5

HARROWING HUNT

"I'm sooo tired," Iseul said with a yawn. She rolled onto her side and wrapped herself tightly in a first-gen ALIBI summer tour blanket.

The team, along with Ha Jun, had been out late using social media to try to track down @LOVE-MY-ALIBI, the screen name of the fan who was posting selfies wearing the jacket.

Every time @LOVE-MY-ALIBI posted a photo of himself in the jacket, the group was off and running, but inevitably showed up right after he'd left. The latest post had them crisscrossing the city from the Tokyo Skytree to Harajuku to the Shinjuku Gyoen National Garden. After navigating their way across the crowded five-way intersection at Shibuya, they returned to their hotel.

"Can't we sleep another hour?" Willow asked, stretched out on the floor with her head on a stack of crumpled maps of the city.

The Tokyo hotel oozed comfort, but ALIBI hadn't even set foot in the bedrooms. Instead, they sat in the living room of their suite tracking the fan on their phones, entering his location into the map. Finally, when they couldn't keep their eyes open any longer, they all crashed on the living room floor. Only Ha Jun had made it to an actual bed, hours before the three girls gave up the search.

Ding.

"I hate that sound," Iseul covered her ears. "Make it go away!"

Ding.

"@LOVE-MY-ALIBI has a new post," Willow said, leaning on one arm.

"Don't look at it," Iseul moaned. "It's just one more boba shop. One more café. One more . . ."

Willow looked at the phone and said, "Theme park."

"We are not going to a theme park," Song Yi said. She dragged herself from the floor to the couch and stretched out. "Forget the jacket. @LOVE-MY-ALIBI can have it. The demon is his now, too." She closed her eyes.

"Good morning, performers!" Ha Jun stepped out of his bedroom to greet them, having rested up a bit. "Everyone get some . . ." He looked around at the empty pizza boxes, chip bags, and bubble tea cups.

"Whoa. I told you to give up the search at midnight." He noticed the girls' drool-stained faces. "No one listens to me," Ha Jun sighed. "As usual."

"We wanted to catch the thief," Song Yi said. She let her brother sit down on the end of the couch next to where her feet lay. But the instant he sat down, she kicked him off. Ha Jun hit the floor with a thunk.

"You also need to perform tonight," he said, brushing himself off before trying to drag his sister off the couch.

"Owww," Song Yi cried. "My fingers still hurt. I won't be able to sing." She hit him with one of the couch cushions.

"You need your fingers to sing?" Ha Jun laughed. He pinned her down with a pillow of his own.

"Nah," Song Yi said. She flipped, and the two of them fell to the floor, knocking over an empty cup.

Ha Jun pulled Song Yi toward him, then turned his hip to execute a major hip throw.

"You've been practicing!" she cheered as she wrapped her legs around his in a modified scissor sweep.

"You think all I do is manage ALIBI?" Ha Jun chuckled, fighting to free his left leg. "The master says, 'A sushi platter is better than tofu.'"

“Wait, I think I kinda know what that means,” Iseul said. Then corrected herself, “Nope. No clue.”

“Uh, can we get serious?” Willow asked. She wedged her way between Ha Jun and Song Yi. “You’ve missed three posts from the fan!” She held up her phone. “He’s here.” Willow pointed at a purple dot. “And we’re here.” The yellow dot.

“He’s across the street from the hotel?” Song Yi said, quickly standing up. She helped Ha Jun get up. “Truce?”

“For now,” Ha Jun agreed, raising two fingers in a peace sign. “Let’s go to the . . .” Ha Jun leaned in toward Willow’s phone. “Mega shop!”

Mega shops were as popular in Japan as they were in South Korea. The multilevel stores had everything from beauty products to clothing stalls to food halls and toys.

“This is practically the same as a theme park,” Willow said as they entered on the main floor.

They wanted to act like they were just surprising the fan, so Ha Jun had given them all concert merch. They wore matching iridescent pearl-colored ALIBI sweatshirts, hoods up, branded sunglasses, and matching baggy sweatpants that said ALIBI WORLD TOUR down the side. Ha Jun wore the same, only his sweatpants were black, and they'd run out of sunglasses, so he pulled a black ALIBI logo beanie down low over his forehead.

"We all look like we bought out the ALIBI gift shop," Song Yi said, catching her reflection in a mirror near the Wonder Market.

"Us and everyone else," Willow said, noting how many people standing in line at the Build-a-Boba counter were dressed pretty much the same.

"ALIBI has the hottest merch in town," Ha Jun said. Then he noticed a child wearing an ALIBI WORD TOUR T-shirt. "*WORD*? Obviously counterfeit!" He reached for his phone. "I'm calling our lawyers."

"Let the kid have his fun," Song Yi said as she swiped the phone out of his hand. "We've got a bigger problem."

She pointed at the floor of the brightly lit aisle of sticker booths and stands selling bead bracelets.

A red sequin glittered up at them.

"They aren't selling anything like this," Song Yi noted. "It's gotta be from my jacket."

Ha Jun went to snatch it, but Iseul held him back. "It'll burn," she warned Ha Jun. She handed him a glass vial and tweezers.

Ha Jun carefully picked up this new sparkle and placed it in the container. "Thanks," he said to Iseul. "I mean, if I touched it, I might not be able to sing later!"

Song Yi laughed. "That'd be doing us all a favor."

Willow checked the purple dot on her phone and reported, "Fan's on the third floor."

There was a line for the escalator, so Ha Jun and Iseul stood at the end. The elevator seemed like a better bet. Willow and Song Yi leapt into the first available car.

When the doors opened, they were in a market space where vendors were selling talismans, crystals, oracle cards, and incense.

"Don't look!" Song Yi dragged Willow.

"My happy place . . ." Willow swooned. Her head spun left and right, taking in all her favorite things. "I could really use a new candle."

"Nope," Song Yi said. There was a glittering glow ahead between stationery and electronics. "Iseul's going to get caught up in electronics, isn't she?"

"We'll come back," Willow said. "Promise me we'll come back?" She reluctantly moved past a booth selling teas and herbs.

"Promise," Song Yi told her. "Look!"

The fan stood on a small stage in front of a growing crowd, holding his phone out with a selfie stick. It was common for malls and markets to have such stages for local performances or, sometimes, bigger groups on publicity junkets.

There weren't any special lights or effects, but the jacket shined as if a spotlight were pointed at it. The sequins cast bright, glistening, ruby-red reflector beams in every direction.

"And that's without the full power," Song Yi moaned. "I want my jacket!"

"Let's get it," Willow said.

Without a plan, they barged toward the stage. It wasn't until they got closer that the crowd closed in around the fan. "Riku! Riku!" they shouted over and over.

"The demon," Song Yi gasped when she saw it peeking out of the fan's pocket. It was no longer the size of a hedgehog. "It looks like a possessed rabbit now."

"Everyone can see it," Iseul said. "Do they think it's a mutant pet?"

The crowd around the fan pushed Song Yi and Willow, shoving them back as Riku continued to take selfies.

They could hear him clearly: "This is Song Yi's jacket! She gave it to me herself!"

The crowd cheered, and the demon-rabbit got fluffier. It was almost as if the crowd knew that if they cheered, Riku's weird pet would grow, as if they wanted to see that happen.

Riku pressed a button on his phone and "Bright City Lights" began to play. He had basic dance skills. His singing voice, though, was exceptional. He riffed off the track, laying down his own harmonies.

"Too bad he's a sneak and a thief," Willow said. "That guy has a great voice."

"Then he should try out for his own group!" Song Yi said, pressing against the crowd, inching toward the stage.

The more Riku sang, the more the oni's face swelled and its fur stretched to fit its growing form.

"If we don't stop it, that bad bunny will become the size of a rotten raccoon!" Song Yi said. "Riku is feeding it with *our* music and fandom!"

"How are we going to stop it?" Willow asked Song Yi.

"You grab the demon; I'll grab the jacket," Song Yi said. "Hopefully, Iseul and Ha Jun will arrive in time to help." She glanced toward the mob of people stepping off the escalator. The louder Riku sang, the more people showed up.

"If one sequin burns your skin, what do you think the whole jacket will do?" Willow asked. "The demon's going to try and keep us away. We can't just grab it."

"Then let's just nab Riku. The demon will have to come along, and that way we can get them both out of here," Song Yi said. "We can figure out the rest later."

Willow raised a hand to stop Song Yi. "There's still one more verse in 'Bright City Lights.' Please, don't do anything yet. I'll be right back." She pushed her way back through the crowd toward the booths that sold crystals, candles, and herbs.

Watching Riku sing her song made Song Yi both proud and furious. She couldn't wait any longer. She had to capture Riku when he hit that last, long dramatic note. It was eight breathless seconds long. That was enough time to knock him down and take him out.

Song Yi still couldn't see Iseul and Ha Jun, and Willow hadn't returned yet. *It has to be now!* she thought. Although she'd never acted alone before, the demon was right in front of her. *It would be so easy*, she assured herself.

As Riku opened his mouth to sing the big note, Song Yi shoved through the crowd.

He was lost in the music, just as she was when she sang this part and the song enveloped her.

Aim for his legs, Song Yi told herself. The scissor kick that she'd used earlier on Ha Jun would be ideal. She'd knock him down without touching the jacket at all.

The note wowed the crowd and gave her the opening she needed. Song Yi finally pushed her way through the front row and leapt, with an explosion of force, onto the stage. Riku's eyes went wide with surprise, but he held the long note.

She swung at him for the scissor kick, but Riku quickly dodged it, all while still singing!

"Impressive," she said out loud, but she knew he couldn't repeat that move. She swept his leg once more, and her assumption was correct. He couldn't deflect her and sing at the same time.

He dropped the final note and skittered away. The selfie stick fell out of his hand. Someone in the crowd grabbed it, and Song Yi could see that they continued to record.

"You only held that note for five seconds, Riku," she said, shaking her head and advancing toward him to strike again. "Bummer. The best fans online can hold that note for at least the full eight." Song Yi got into position for a double leg takedown. "I usually do nine seconds, ten if the crowd moves me."

"Show-off!" Riku said, evading her fighting moves. He growled in a deep, rough, echoing voice. "My fame will be greater than yours! I'll dominate the world."

"That's not you, Riku. It's the oni in the jacket." She circled him, half-crouched, and prepared to pounce. "Take off the jacket and you'll be free."

"Fame brings fortune," Riku—still under the control of the oni—recited, curling into himself and shaking. "Fame brings fortune."

Song Yi prepared to make another swipe at his legs when Iseul suddenly pounced onto the stage. Riku froze, knowing he'd soon be overpowered. The fans looked on in anticipation, some recording the action with their phones.

"Song Yi! Wait!" Iseul carried a personal safety alarm. When activated, the popular device created an ear-splitting sound. At Song Yi's questioning glance, Iseul explained, "Sorry I'm late. Had to shop at several electronic booths! I modified this basic alarm to create a focused sonic pulse." She grinned.

"It'll stun the demon without touching Riku or the jacket."

Iseul raised a finger over the control as Willow high-jumped onto the stage to join them. "I bought an obsidian crystal pyramid to ground the demon's energy. The runes on the base will magnetically bind the oni to the stone." She showed them the baseball-sized black pyramid. "The demon's energy will be absorbed and it'll return to being just a regular pet. Then we can dispose of the pyramid and 'Bye-bye, demon.'" She added a side note: "I bought the small pyramid first, then had to return it because it wasn't strong enough. Then—get this—I couldn't find the receipt."

Song Yi rolled her eyes, then shouted their rallying cry as they formed a circle around Riku. "It's time to reveal the truth."

"Hey!" Riku swept his hand toward the audience as if this were all part of a show. "Look! It's ALIBI!"

At first, no one believed him—the concert merch was a great disguise—but slowly a ripple traveled through the audience. The cheers grew as people recognized Iseul, Willow, and Song Yi in their sweatshirts.

And as the cheers grew, the demon grew.

"Shhh!" Song Yi tried to calm the crowd.

"No clapping."

"No shouting," Willow added.

"No stomping," Iseul tried.

With the fans shrieking for them to perform, Riku leaned in and said, "And now it's my turn to say it . . . 'Bye-bye, ALIBI!'" He leapt off the back of the stage. "See ya later!" In a flash, he was swallowed up by the mob of people getting off the escalator. The red jacket, the demon, *and* the fan had slipped away.

"Sing," Ha Jun called to the group from the side of the stage. "If the fans know you're ALIBI, you can't be doing demon detective work. Let Riku go for now," he told them. "In this moment, you gotta be *you*!"

"Great line for a song," Song Yi said as any hope of knocking Riku down, stunning him with sound, and trapping him in a crystal pyramid disappeared.

Ha Jun ran to the back of the stage and flicked on a light switch. Suddenly, the stage glowed with bright multicolored can lights, and an instant later, a fog machine he'd found kicked on, too. "Spontaneous concert promo—let's get those clicks!"

Iseul began to live stream. Willow did a backward flip.

Song Yi belted out an eleven-second note.

CHAPTER 6

TRICKING THE TRICKSTER

"I can't believe we didn't catch Riku," Song Yi said as the makeup artist brushed on a ruby eye shadow that matched her kimono. ALIBI fans had gushed about the kimonos on social media, the governor had reposted it, and now kimono sales were up all over Japan. Way up.

The makeup artist and the hairdresser were hired by the producer. They'd been sworn to such deep levels of secrecy that Song Yi and the others weren't allowed to ask their names. They weren't there to be friends, as much as the girls might have wanted them to; they were there to make the group look pro and to forget anything they might hear.

"He's a tricky one," Iseul said, boots propped up on the coffee table once again.

In the mirror, Song Yi nodded her head in agreement. "This is not going to be easy," she said.

Willow hadn't arrived yet. She said there was something important she needed to do first.

"I bet Willow's at the Mega shop buying sage and a crystal ball," Song Yi said. The makeup artist finished and moved aside to let the hairdresser spray a new product they were paid to endorse. It smelled nice but was stickier than Song Yi liked. She thought it was a little unnatural that her hair didn't even move during the dance numbers.

As the clock struck 5:21, Song Yi moved out of the stylist's chair to let Iseul sit down. It was one minute past time to take out the curlers in Iseul's hair and freshen the colors with a sweep of gel.

"These early start times really get in the way of my dinner plans," Song Yi said, grabbing a sushi roll from a small wheeled cart near the couch and stuffing it into her mouth. Then she grabbed two salmon hand rolls and sat where Iseul had warmed the cushion.

"Want to know the time in binary?" Iseul asked Song Yi. "If we convert the twenty-four-hour format of 17:21, then 17 divided by 2 is 8 with a remainder of 1, and we—"

"You took too long!" Song Yi laughed, pointing at the clock. "Now it's 5:22."

"I'll start over," Iseul said.

"Nah, that's okay." Song Yi picked up Iseul's digital notebook from the coffee table. "Look here." She held up the notebook for Iseul's face recognition.

"In," she said as she opened the page where Iseul had been keeping track of the mystery.

Iseul was an amazing notetaker. She didn't miss a single detail, and where there were information gaps, she highlighted a few key questions. Like:

How did Riku get the jacket?

If Minato felt powerful in the jacket, what did Riku feel?

How big can this oni grow?

"Good notes," Song Yi said. She turned the tablet toward Iseul. "And I like this initial drawing you made of the oni."

"I drew it just like I remembered it," Iseul said. "I even added Yumi Kondo in the corner. I didn't see her, but you told me about the way she stared at the hidden back door to the studio."

Song Yi nodded and rotated the tablet back to herself. Iseul had accurately captured the way Yumi Kondo looked the day that they got the jackets, when Song Yi went back into the studio for her bag.

The way Yumi Kondo stood, not reacting to Song Yi's presence, was strange. *What if . . . ?*

The door to the dressing room opened.

Ha Jun bounded in. Literally. He did a showstopping Xtreme Martial Arts flash kick, bounding forward, then performing a backflip with a kick at the top of his rotation. "HA-YA!" he cried. "Ha Jun is here!"

Song Yi snorted, pretending that his entrance wasn't impressive. "I give it a five out of ten," she said with a fake yawn. "Iseul?"

"Uh, you mean ten out of ten?" Iseul questioned Song Yi's vote. "Can *you* do that move, Song Yi?"

Song Yi crossed her arms. "Willow does our gymnastics."

"Did I tell you how this arena was built for the Tokyo Olympics?" Ha Jun laughed. "I'm prepping for my Olympic premiere one day."

"You're weird," Song Yi told her brother.

"No, you are," he replied.

"No time for this," Willow said, coming into the dressing room, carrying a large shopping bag. She'd done her own makeup, braided her own hair, and added new sapphire-colored bows.

"Those bows are growing like the demon," Iseul said. "Weren't they smaller last night?"

"@ALI-FAN-ABI-2001 suggested I make them bigger so the last arena rows can see them without binoculars." Willow flicked her braid. "Of course, if I did that, I'd swim in ribbon, but this size should be better for viewing."

"More clicks!" Ha Jun said. "Awesome idea." He turned to his sister. "You should do something nice for the fans, too."

"How about I just save the fans from a growing demon," she said with sarcasm. "Is that good for you?"

"You're impossible," he replied.

"No, you're impossible," Song Yi told her brother.

"Wanna see what I bought?" Willow asked. She set the bag on the floor and pulled out the tissue paper. "The paper can be planted to grow flowers," she said, carefully folding it before setting it aside. "If the oni grows any larger, the obsidian triangle won't be enough to adhere to its spirit. We need something more powerful." She added, "I found the perfect thing."

Iseul's hair and makeup were done. She came over to look while the glam team quickly packed up and left the room.

Willow swept a large cloak out of her bag and swung it around her shoulders.

"You look like a wizard!" Iseul said.

"You can't wear that!" Ha Jun almost choked on a piece of sushi. He spat salmon into his hand. "Crushes the vibe!"

"Oh, I'm not wearing it," Willow said, circling Ha Jun. "You are."

"Me?" He tossed the sushi and drank a sip of water. "You're mistaken."

Willow flipped the cloak around his shoulders and fastened the tie. Song Yi held back a laugh.

"It's a Japanese black binding cloth!" she explained.

"The woman who sold it to me called it an obsidian grid cloth." Willow took Ha Jun by the shoulders and spun him around. "Obsidian is still the best stone for gluing itself to a demon." She opened the folds of the cloak to show the others. "While there aren't actual stones in the fabric, the black color will do the same job. The grid design represents the core function of the stone, so if we toss this over the demon, it'll be unable to move."

"We?" Ha Jun asked, suddenly excited to wear the cloak. "I'm the one in the cloak with the smooth moves."

"Stick close by us, though," Willow said. "I imagine it'll take all of us to cloak the demon!"

She reached into her bag again and pulled out a golden lantern with a strange alphabetic design etched into the glass. "The cloth won't hold the demon for long, so we'll need to shrink it back to mouse size and transfer its essence into a holding device." Willow handed the lantern to Iseul. "Can you fix this old lantern up?"

"Can I?!" Iseul's eyes widened with excitement. She spun the lantern by its thin handle. "I'm going to rewire the LED core and install a capacitor module. Then I'll create a copper circuit and use that obsidian pyramid that you bought yesterday as a grounding mechanism—"

"Whoa." Ha Jun stopped her. "You have only nine minutes before stage time. You can't possibly do all that now."

"We don't have to do it right now," Willow told him. "Riku and the oni aren't at the show tonight." She dug into the bag one last time and pulled out her cellphone. She showed Riku's social. "He's at an idol lounge."

Riku was live-streaming himself wearing the red jacket and dancing at a preshow club. The demon, now as big as a Shiba Inu, a medium-size Japanese dog, stood by his side. He sang the words to "Wild

Wild" while petting the demon's head, lovingly scratching it between the horns.

"I scoured the internet," Iseul said. "ALIBI fans seem to think the demon is a holograph and that it has something to do with our show. Riku keeps telling everyone that the jacket is Song Yi's, so I guess they figure the demon belongs to her, too. Oddly, it's kind of becoming our mascot."

"We can sell plushies," Ha Jun suggested.

"NO!" the girls all shouted at him.

"Worthless demon." Ha Jun frowned.

"If we take what we learned at the mall," Song Yi said, "it seems to follow logically that the oni can grow outside of the arena. It feeds on our fame anytime an excited group of our fans are dancing and singing along."

"Hopefully not as fast as it would if it were near us." Iseul raised crossed fingers. "We'll do our thing here, alert security to keep Riku out, and see if we can catch up with Riku and the demon after the show."

Song Yi sighed. "I *really* want my jacket back."

"Sure, we'd all love to see the jackets on stage, but did you see the sales of pink pants, teal skirts, and black shorts?" Ha Jun asked. "Like the kimonos, your off-duty clothes are fire!"

"Ugh," said Song Yi, who cherished the quiet moments. "We'll never be able to go out unrecognized again."

"No worries, sis," Ha Jun assured her. He swished the black cloak around himself like a superhero. Or a villain. "We're going out for dinner and I have a plan."

There was a second prerecorded video break in the show schedule. It was after the song that Song Yi wrote for Willow called "Superstitious Wishes." The song hadn't gotten the traction of the others, but it was Song Yi's favorite show moment.

Iseul had rigged up the most amazing tech stage props to honor Willow. When they danced, the whole arena swelled with the soft light of imitation candles, and fresh flowers dropped into the audience for added ambience. The faint scent of a garden's morning dew was wafted through the crowd.

This was a true "you had to be there" moment for the fans in the arena.

ALIBI light sticks were programmed to flicker along until the last few notes of the song, then the arena plunged into darkness and the video started rolling.

ALIBI took to the wings to rest and have some water.

While the first video, or "VCR," break was the group's origin story, this one focused on the tour. It was common for K-pop fans to travel to multiple shows, so the video previewed other stops on the tour and advertised sponsor hotels, brands, and shops on several large screens at once.

While the video played a short clip Ha Jun had taken after they were recognized in their ALIBI gear, Song Yi, Iseul, and Willow stayed close to Ha Jun backstage.

"Why do I have to wear this fashion monstrosity if Riku isn't even in the arena?" he complained about the cloak.

"You never know when you might need it," Willow said. "Plus, wizarding might be your new look!" She peeked out to see the rehearsal bloopers of Iseul stumbling over dance moves. The audience laughed.

The next video flickered with a funny story about when they all went out to Iseul's goat farm. Willow had wanted to do goat yoga, but the goats acted out and things got really silly. They kept jumping on top of Willow and stepping on her head. The laughter in the arena grew as a cute, speckled baby goat tried to eat Willow's hair.

"I hope the demon doesn't feed on laughter," Willow remarked. "It will be bigger than the sun after the part where the goat chases Song Yi."

"I still have nightmares," Song Yi said, watching the video as if seeing the story for the first time. She laughed quietly as she watched the goats chase her down. Iseul and the others had seen this video too many times to count, and still it was a favorite.

Then Song Yi caught a glimpse of something she hadn't noticed before. It was Iseul gazing at the goats with a look of love. Somehow Iseul adored these goats even though they'd been chasing down her friends and eating their hair. They were cute, but also wicked, creatures. But these goats were more than farm creatures to Iseul. They were . . . *OH!*

"Oh! OH! OHHHH!" Song Yi suddenly exclaimed. "Where is Yumi Kondo?"

"Probably still looking around for your jacket," Ha Jun said. "We don't need her tonight. There's no reason for her to come and fit you all when Song Yi's jacket is missing."

"We *do* need her!" Song Yi's voice was tight. "Can you get her here?"

"Before the video ends?" Ha Jun snorted.

"You're the wizard," Song Yi said, gesturing toward the cloak. "Do magic."

Ha Jun swished the cloak. "Abracadabra, one very self-absorbed, slightly freaky, fashion designer coming right up!" He paused before whisking himself away to say, "Do well and come back."

"YOU do well and come back," Song Yi said, knowing that he'd never get back before they had to perform the next song.

Song Yi's big announcement would have to wait.

CHAPTER 7

THE GOVERNOR'S GUILT

"I have no idea where Yumi Kondo has disappeared to," Ha Jun said when they gathered in the dressing room the next night. He realized how that sounded and added, "I mean, she hasn't disappeared-disappeared, *probably*. I just couldn't find her after the show."

Iseul leaned back on the dressing room couch with her feet on the coffee table. Song Yi gave her a look of disapproval, but germs were not on Iseul's radar. "Do you need us to help you investigate?" Iseul asked Ha Jun.

"No," Ha Jun insisted. "We have twenty-four more hours in Tokyo. She'll turn up eventually. What's the deal, sis?"

"I just need to talk to her," Song Yi said cryptically. "I'll wait."

"You keep saying that, *noona*." Ha Jun raised his eyes to the ceiling and asked impatiently, "Why not just tell us all what it's about?"

"Yumi Kondo has to be there," Song Yi replied.

"You're irritating," Ha Jun told his sister.

"No, you are."

"Hey, before we get started in this verbal ping-pong game you two play," Iseul said, "our dinner guests are waiting at the restaurant."

"We have an hour for dinner," Ha Jun said, "then a quick trip back here to the dressing room. The stylists will be ready to roll." He pointed at the clock. "Two hours to showtime." And before Iseul could say anything, he told her, "One-zero-zero-zero-one, zero-zero-zero-zero-zero in binary."

"You're truly the best manager ever," she gushed.

"Just doing my job," he said. "Now get ready to run. 'Project AVF: Avoid the Fans' is about to begin."

What would have been a ten-minute walk to the restaurant became fifteen minutes in an unmarked white van in traffic.

"We can't get delayed by autographs or photos," Ha Jun said as the group's Nippon Budokan security detail stood by the restaurant door. "I posted a decoy restaurant on ALIBI's social." He glanced down the empty street. "Looks like it worked."

"Proud of you, brother, but don't let tonight's successes go to your head. You gotta find Yumi Kondo."

"Yeah, you keep saying that, *noona*," he moaned.

The governor and her husband stood just inside the restaurant door. It was unclear who was greeting whom and what the protocol should be. The K-pop group wanted to pay respect to the governor, but the governor was also clearly excited to meet them.

Iseul set the example. She bowed at a 30-degree angle, politely and respectfully. Song Yi, Willow, and Ha Jun imitated the move with their hands down at their sides, eyes lowered, and held the pose for two seconds before slowly rising to standing.

"*Hajimemashite*," Iseul greeted. "Nice to meet you."

This was the Japanese way.

The governor responded with a shallower bow, more like a head nod, and offered her hand for a Western-style handshake.

"Nice to meet you as well."

With the greetings out of the way, the governor and her husband welcomed ALIBI and Ha Jun into a beautiful room with low tables and tatami flooring, the soft mats used in traditional Japanese rooms.

Song Yi took her place on a *zabuton*, a comfy floor cushion, next to the governor.

“I am pleased you enjoyed the kimonos,” the governor said.

“We love them,” Willow replied. “And they came just in time.”

“What do you mean?” the governor asked.

Iseul elbowed Willow. The missing jacket was not common knowledge, so there was no way that the governor would know the kimonos were a substitute for the real costumes.

“Just that we wanted something cultural to show our respect,” Willow said.

“I see . . .” A wrinkle formed just above the governor’s brow.

Song Yi, attuned to seeing things that others did not, wondered whether the governor suspected something about the mystery. She decided to slip in a few questions.

“I love Japanese fashion,” she said. “Do you have a favorite designer?”

Ah, that wrinkle deepened. “I do,” the governor said.

“In fact, it was the governor who suggested Yumi Kondo,” Ha Jun said, adding a new clue to the overall mystery.

“It was?” Iseul didn’t have her tablet, but it looked like she was itching to write that down.

"She's my sister," the governor said.

Song Yi's eyes got big. She knew Yumi Kondo had a brother, but a sister was a surprise.

Ha Jun spoke before Song Yi could. "Do you happen to know where she is, like, right now?"

"I don't, but I could text her," the governor suggested.

"PLEASE!" All of ALIBI said together.

The governor picked up her phone and, a moment later, replied, "She's not answering."

"I'll ask the restaurant to present dinner," Ha Jun said, one eye on his smartwatch. "The girls are on a tight schedule."

"Understood," the governor said. While Ha Jun went to advise the servers, she leaned over and whispered to her husband, who suddenly rose from the table.

"I'll meet you at the show," he said, leaving the room before they'd placed the order.

Song Yi's eyes followed him out of the room.

"I asked my husband to leave us all alone for a private conversation," the governor said. "I never intended for kimonos to fly off our shelves. I wanted it to be the jackets designed by my sister. I have long dreamed of an opportunity for her like this one." She sighed. "I understand that one jacket is missing."

"We hope to have it back by tomorrow's show," Song Yi said.

A server in a shiny gray kimono kneeled and laid a starter of sakura salmon crudo before each guest. Ha Jun flagged him down as he was about to leave and quietly whispered in his ear. A moment later, the server returned with a tofu puff for Willow, then hustled away again.

"That's good to hear," the governor said. "How can I help?"

"You already know," Song Yi said.

The governor nodded, then raised her phone. She sent a quick text and then, not a second later, Yumi Kondo entered the dining room.

She didn't bow or greet in a traditional way. Instead, she blurted, "You know, right? I knew you'd figure it out."

"Huh?" Willow asked.

"I think she's talking to Song Yi," Iseul said.

"Oh," Willow said.

"How'd you know?" Yumi Kondo said, sitting down on the cushion that the governor's husband had left open.

“The video of Iseul and her goats,” Song Yi admitted. “The way Iseul watched those goats reminded me of the way you stood in the studio, watching Minato leave through the back door.” She added, “You weren’t actually watching him. You were thinking about the secret pet oni you had waiting back there.”

“I told her getting that *thing* was a terrible idea!” the governor said. “But she said having it around helped her self-esteem and confidence.”

“Always an issue,” Yumi Kondo said with downcast eyes. “I just never believe in myself.”

“I’d have never guessed,” Willow said. “The studio . . .”

“The eye scanner . . .” Iseul put in.

“The NDAs . . .” Ha Jun said.

“All part of the show,” Song Yi told them. “Yumi Kondo puts on a good show to look like a famous designer.”

“I am so far behind here,” Willow said. “Song Yi, what is going on?”

“I realized—” Song Yi had to stop while the server brought the second dish, a charcoal-grilled Wagyu tenderloin for each guest, and a vegetable kaiseki plate for Willow. When he left the room again, she finished, “The oni is Yumi Kondo’s pet.”

"Tommy," she said.

Ha Jun couldn't help himself. He laughed. "Seriously? That's the cutest demon name I've ever heard."

"Named after a popular American actor, Tom Cruise," she replied. "I love action movies." She shook her head to get back on track. "My designs weren't selling, and my social media had no followers. I was lost."

"I wore her designs to every political event," the governor said. "Nothing helped."

"A person—I don't know who—slipped a note to me in a café telling me to come to the back of the shop. They said they could make all my troubles disappear." Yumi Kondo sighed. "I was desperate."

The governor took her sister's hand for support.

"There was a little wee baby dormouse with tiny little horns in a cage and a QR with a price on top. It was so adorable! I sent the requested money and took Tommy home." She had that look again, the one Song Yi recognized as love for a pet. "And it was amazing having this new pet! I felt more confident when Tommy was around. My dreams became clearer, and they began to come true."

"That's what Minato said when he put on the jacket," Iseul reminded them.

"The oni lets you see fame and fortune, but it's the demon's fame and fortune, not yours," Song Yi said.

"The dream felt real to me," Yumi Kondo said.

Dessert came to the table: yuzu meringue with matcha ice cream for everyone.

"I didn't know it could let itself out of the cage," Yumi Kondo said. "And I didn't know it would grow."

That explained the look of both love and concern that Song Yi had seen on her face that day in the studio.

"Have you seen how big it is now?" Iseul pulled up Riku's social and turned the screen to face Yumi Kondo. "Tommy's the size of a horse!"

"That's not good," Yumi Kondo said, blinking back a tear. "I can't understand what happened. I loved Tommy so! Still do." She frowned. "I hoped the person who originally gave the oni to me has answers for us. I've been searching throughout Tokyo," she explained. "But there's no trace."

While Yumi Kondo leaned against her sister for a hug, ALIBI put their heads together.

"Whoever left the demon is one more mystery to solve," Iseul whispered to her friends, while sneaking a spoonful of Ha Jun's matcha.

"We better leave that mystery for another day," Song Yi replied. She stood at the table and said loudly, "It's time for the show. We need to go, but we promise that this conversation will stay private."

"Do we need to sign a new NDA?" Ha Jun asked as they all prepared to leave.

"No," Song Yi said. "But I am now realizing the one we signed at the studio, vowing that we wouldn't talk about what we saw, was about more than revealing the jackets to the public. It was to protect Yumi Kondo from our talking about *anything* we might have seen in the studio that day."

"I suppose I had an instinct about Tommy after all," Yumi Kondo agreed. "Total secrecy felt necessary."

"And this conversation needs to stay private as well," Song Yi said. "ALIBI will find the demon and dispatch it. And then we will wear your jackets on stage, because your designs are wonderful. You don't need a demon to bring you fame and fortune. You just need to know how great you are without it."

Yumi Kondo nodded.

"ALIBI will help you," Willow assured Yumi Kondo. "But you gotta be nicer to Minato."

"It was part of Tommy's effect on me," Yumi Kondo said. "Famous people are always cruel to their workers."

"That is not true," Iseul insisted. "Not true at all."

"I see that now," Yumi Kondo bowed low, in a traditional apologetic way. "I'm so sorry. So very sorry."

Full of food and loaded down with questions, ALIBI made it to the dressing room on time.

While Song Yi was getting her hair done, Iseul pulled out the tablet. "Why didn't the demon influence Song Yi? She wore the jacket when Tommy was hiding in it."

Willow spun the obsidian pyramid in her hand. "I've been thinking about that," she said. "This oni helps people visualize their dreams: Minato wants fortune. Riku wants fame. Yumi Kondo wants both." She paused, considering, then asked, "What if Song Yi already has everything she wants?"

"I don't *want* fame or fortune," Song Yi said.

"Which is why the jacket didn't work on you," Willow replied.

The makeup artist swiped red sparkling eye shadow over Song Yi's lids.

"I have more than I ever dreamed," she said. "Friends, family, a great life!" She missed her parents and wished they were there to see what she and Ha Jun had accomplished, but their grandparents had been there to witness it, and that helped a lot.

"The demon can only grow so much on the illusions it creates," Willow said. "It needs Song Yi. She's the secret to growing and gaining strength. When it saw us perform in the fashion studio, the demon realized that it grew when ALIBI received applause." She swapped seats with Song Yi and the hairstylist straightened her bows. "If we can't catch it, we need to end the applause that's feeding it."

"How would we do that?!" Iseul snorted. "You want to hush fifteen thousand fans?"

"What else can we do?" Willow asked.

The question hung in the air, because at that moment, Ha Jun burst into the dressing room. "We have a message from the producer!"

"Are you sweating?" Song Yi asked.

"Yes!" He waved his hands under his armpits. "And not from a workout. It's bad news." Ha Jun read a text directly from his phone.

"You must catch the oni immediately. If you don't do it before you leave Tokyo, I will cancel the rest of the tour. It's growing too big and must be stopped."

Having delivered the message, Ha Jun slumped his shoulders. "We can't cancel the tour! Think of the fans!"

Willow stood and placed the obsidian pyramid on the coffee table, next to the dark cloak and the lantern. "We only have two shows left. This won't be easy."

Iseul wrapped her hands around herself and shivered. "What if we can't do it?"

"We have to try," Song Yi said. "What else can we do?"

The concert was a horrible mess.

First, it started late.

The girls were at the lift in time, but there was a problem: The button was stuck. It wouldn't budge. An engineer arrived at three minutes past the hour, but she couldn't diagnose the problem. In the end, at sixteen minutes after the start time, the girls ran onto the stage from the wings instead of rising directly to center stage as they always did.

Because of the mishap and the clock ticking in Ha Jun's head, he forgot to say "Do well and come back."

And it slipped Song Yi's mind to say "We've got this."

During "Wild Wild," Song Yi counted wrong. "One. Two. Three. Five . . ." and that mistake meant that she threw off the choreography. The sliding steps were off a beat, and someone in the audience shouted, "Go left!" to her.

In "Bright City Lights," Iseul got wrapped up in her kimono and tripped. When she was sprawled out on the stage floor, Willow nearly stepped on her. They both tried to make it look like new dance steps, but the fans knew better. Thousands of cameras recorded their mistakes, and the girls knew without looking that the internet was already buzzing with questions about the performance.

At the first video break, Ha Jun brought the girls water and energy chews. "What is going on out there?" he asked. "I've never seen you three like this. Not ever!"

"We've never had so much pressure," Willow said. "And there was not even time for a soothing face mask!"

"We don't need to see Riku's live feed to know that the demon is growing off our fans' applause," Iseul said.

"So, are you *trying* to disappoint the fans?" Ha Jun asked. "I know you thought that a silent concert without applause was impossible. Is this your weird new plan? If the fans hate you, the demon will shrink?"

"Not intentionally," Song Yi said. She tilted her head. "But would that work?"

“I could botch the landing on my flip,” Willow suggested.

“What if I glitch out the light sticks?” Iseul asked.

“Pull yourselves together,” Ha Jun told them. He removed the obsidian cloak and set it aside. “Put on a good show for your fans. We’ll deal with the oni later.”

“By the time the show ends, the demon will be the size of a rhinoceros!” Willow exclaimed.

After some thought, Song Yi said, “Our minds are too preoccupied with how to stop the demon. It’s causing us to make mistakes. Ha Jun, you have to cancel the rest of the show.”

“What are you talking about?” The governor had come running up to them. “You can’t cancel the show. So many people bought tickets!”

“We can’t risk the demon’s feeding off the applause and cheers,” Iseul said. “The mistakes in the performance are a sign: We’re not focused. This is not our best show.”

“Might be our worst,” Willow suggested.

“Cancel the show, Ha Jun,” Song Yi said. He stared at her, shaking his head. “If you won’t, I will.” Before Ha Jun could stop her, Song Yi ran out onto the stage and waved to the lighting booth to raise the spotlights.

"If you couldn't tell," she told the crowd, "we're having a rough night. Forgive us, but we're going to end the show here and invite you all to come back tomorrow."

Ha Jun jogged out onto the stage next to her carrying a portable mic. "Just kidding!" Covering his microphone, he leaned toward his sister. "The arena is sold out. We can't fit tonight's audience in with tomorrow's."

Willow and Iseul came onto the stage, escorting the governor with them. The audience applauded respectfully.

"Governor," Iseul said, "if we promise the best show that ALIBI has ever given . . . will you help us find a BIGGER stadium for tomorrow night?"

At that, the crowd cheered in a frenzy. Whispers of "The best show ever" echoed through the audience.

The governor looked offstage, caught Yumi Kondo's eye, and received a nod. "Yes!" she said, taking the microphone from Ha Jun. "Yes. And I promise we will have a huge surprise for you. New costumes by my sister, fashion designer Yumi Kondo!"

"You can't promise that," Ha Jun whispered to the governor. "We don't know how to find . . ." he couldn't say it with all those cameras on him. "You-know-who and you-know-what."

"You will," the governor replied off mic with full confidence. Then she spoke into the microphone: "I believe ALIBI can do anything."

"Maybe not *anything*, but we've got to try." Song Yi waved to the audience and shouted, "See you all tomorrow!"

ALIBI, the governor, Yumi Kondo, and Ha Jun met offstage while the audience filed out of the arena.

Without the stress of performing and counting steps, Song Yi finally had a plan. "We need to invite Riku to join us onstage."

"Yes!" they all agreed.

"I'll put it on our socials," Iseul said. "We'll find him fast."

"I'll change our choreography for 'Bright City Lights' to include Iseul's modified lantern and Yumi Kondo's jackets!" Willow said. She nipped the cloak away from Ha Jun. "I need this back."

"How do you know the demon will come?" Ha Jun asked Song Yi.

"Huge arena, huge crowd, more applause. The demon is using Riku as a vessel, but the demon needs to feed." Song Yi had no doubts. "They'll both be there for their own selfish reasons."

CHAPTER 8

SUPER ARENA STAGE

The concert the next night moved from the Nippon Budokan to the Saitama Super Arena.

Ha Jun was disappointed to leave his Olympic stories behind, but where the old arena held space for about 14,000 fans, the Super Arena could hold nearly 40,000 people. It was one of the biggest venues in Japan, and many of the great K-pop groups had already performed there. This was a step up for ALIBI and, to be honest, a huge boon for a cheer-devouring demon to expand its fame.

The dressing room at the Super Arena was enormous. There were three distinct zones for the performers to get ready: hair and makeup, wardrobe, and a seating area with three couches, one for each of them. Plus, there was a leather armchair for Ha Jun.

Ha Jun kicked his feet up on an electronic footrest and pointed at the dressing room clock, which he'd brought from Nippon Budokan. "It's 5:30 post meridian, or 17:30 on a twenty-four-hour schedule . . ."

"Binary time: hour one-zero-zero-zero-one, minute one-one-one-one-zero," Iseul said with a laugh.

A security guard popped his head into the large private suite and announced, "Your guest is here." He knew the group because, just like a lot of the staff, he'd come over with them from Nippon Budokan. "Good luck tonight." He closed the door.

"The show starts now that Riku is here," Song Yi told them.

"He's early," Ha Jun said with a nod. He was wearing a dark suit, but not the cloak. That, along with the other tools they'd need, were hidden onstage.

"Depends on which show you're here for," Song Yi replied. "For this one, Riku is on time." Luckily, they were all ready to perform. Getting ready went a lot faster when you could use three prep stations instead of taking turns at one.

Riku entered the room, flanked by the arena's private security. He wore Song Yi's red jacket, which looked even more sparkling than when Song Yi saw it in the studio. The demon's glow was now enmeshed in the jacket, and even though the demon no longer fit into the pocket, the jacket and the oni were one in spirit and energy.

Riku looked different from the last time they'd seen him in person. His eyes had turned the same golden color as the demon's. A stubble of beard grew in random patches across his chin. He also smelled very strongly of rotten eggs and a strange kind of perfume. It was hard for Song Yi to get too close without plugging her nose.

The demon, alongside Riku, hadn't grown much since they'd seen it online the night before, possibly because of the canceled show. The oni was about the size of a large horse, its horns curled like a ram's. The odd way it pressed back into its hind legs made it look like it was trying to stand upright.

"Welcome," Song Yi said, ushering them both into the dressing room. "We are excited to host @LOVE-MY-ALIBI at our final show."

"The invitation said I'd been chosen by a social media lottery," Riku said. His demonic eyes scanned the room. "We all know that is not true. You want me gone, and I want the same for you. Before this show is over, your fans will be mine, and ALIBI won't exist."

"Appreciate the honesty," Willow said. "Let the takedown begin."

"Tokyo Takedown," Riku repeated, placing a tender hand on the demon's head looming over him. "I like it. Yes, we shall begin."

"So now that the purpose of this gathering is clear," Ha Jun said, trying to keep his voice steady and calm, "let's get you all over to the lift and up on the stage." He pointed to the wall clock. "Tick tock. It's time."

Song Yi, Willow, and Iseul wore their off-duty look. If all went well, they'd be wearing their designer jackets by the end of the show. If it didn't . . . well, Song Yi didn't want to think about the alternative.

ALIBI crowded onto the below-stage platform with Riku. It was tight (and smelly) with both Riku and the demon on the lift. Song Yi found herself mashed up against the demon-horse's left flank.

Willow coughed from the smell and turned her head away.

"You get used to it on a farm," Iseul told her. "I've smelled worse."

"Do well and come back!" Ha Jun called out, as if this show were just like any other. He put more emphasis on the "come back" part than he usually did.

The lights in the arena clicked off. An expectant darkness filled the space. The crowd hushed.

Just as she always did, Song Yi raised her hands, the cue for the spotlights, and said, "We've got this."

"Do I get to say something inspirational?" Riku asked with a chuckle.

"NO!" all three members of ALIBI said at the same time.

BOOM.

Three spotlights burst on, and the music started to play.

Riku didn't know it, but the order of songs had changed. Willow suggested that since Riku knew the words to "Bright City Lights," and that was the song that had the best dance steps (including the "spinny thing," aka "the killing part"), it made sense to take out the demon with that number, and to get it done first—before the oni had a chance to grow any bigger.

The audience gasped at the first notes of the song.

"This isn't your usual playlist," Riku said with a suspicious glare. The lift was nearly flush with the stage and level enough to step out into the lights.

"We knew you liked this song," Willow said.

"We heard you perform it," Iseul said.

"It's fantastic," Riku told them. "The clapping and shouts will bring me power." The demon nodded. Riku rubbed his hands along the sequins of the jacket. Song Yi noticed a glistening red dot fall onto the lift.

She couldn't grab it, not without burning her hand, so she left it there.

ALIBI, with their special guests, stepped into a perfectly matched inward rotation. Riku didn't just know the songs; he knew every dance move. He truly was a devoted fan.

Having gotten used to the group in street clothes, the audience cheered when the spotlights highlighted their basic outfits, causing the demon to grow a little.

The crowd seemed to accept the horned horse as a kind of prop. "It's a *magical* night," explained Song Yi. We welcome @LOVE-MY-ALIBI and his animal friend to the stage."

Everyone applauded for Riku and began shouting, "Horned horse!"

"Just got you forty thousand new viewers for your page," Song Yi told Riku and the demon. "Too bad you won't be able to enjoy them!"

"Oh, I am *enjoying* every fan." The voice didn't come from Riku that time. It came from the horse, from the demon himself. "I'm unstoppable!"

The audience sang the song's words, "Bags packed, ticket booked . . . bright city!"

Riku kept up with ALIBI's steps, in perfect sync, until the big dance break. He broke away from the girls, stopped, and stood statue-still in the center of the stage with his arms raised as the fans stomped and cheered. The girls watched in horror as the demon quickly doubled in size.

"ALIBI! Now!" Ha Jun called from stage left. He tossed the obsidian pyramid to Willow, who caught it like a sports star. They all knew the little pyramid wouldn't do much, but they hoped it'd be enough to break the bond between the oni and Riku, if only for a moment. Maybe Riku was still somewhere in his body, and with a pause in the oni's possession, he could free himself.

This was phase one: a test to determine what kind of power they were dealing with.

It was all choreographed so that no one in the crowd would realize that while ALIBI was giving a great performance, they were also attempting to dispatch a demon.

While the audience was focused on Riku, Iseul grabbed three matching cloaks from the back of the stage. There was only one with the obsidian grid woven into the fabric; the others were fakes that Yumi Kondo had whipped up.

Song Yi took the cloak with the grid and moved to the center of the stage next to Riku.

When the girls swept the cloaks around their shoulders, they truly looked like magicians ready for their lounge act. Only this wasn't any normal magic show . . .

Song Yi hadn't realized that Riku would need to stop dancing in order to channel the massive waves of demonic power fueled by the huge audience. They thought they'd need to hold him down, so Willow had prepped a crazy choreographed move to knock him over, but this was going to be easier.

Willow tossed Song Yi the pyramid and they formed a triangle around Riku. The girls passed the pyramid from person to person, all while spinning around him.

"One. Two. Toss. Left," Song Yi recited to herself. She spun twice in four-beat counts, then got the pyramid thrown to her again.

"Riku!" Song Yi shouted to the fan. "Are you able to break free?"

"Why would I want to?" he called back to her. The horse was now the size of three horses. Bigger than two stacked rhinoceroses. And it had begun to stand on its back legs now, too: a mighty beast towering over the girls on the stage.

"We knew this might not work," Willow said when it was her turn. She pelted the demon in the head with the pyramid. It bounced off its left horn. "Worth a try," she said, shrugging.

The audience was in an ecstatic fever singing the lyrics, dancing, and encouraging the oni to grow as if this were all part of ALIBI's "best show ever."

The "killing part" began. When ALIBI spun around, they would usually change quickly from the kimonos into their street clothes. This time, though, they were going to spin the steps while capturing the demon in a cage.

The dance formation moved in toward the demon. It was obvious that Riku no longer held any power. He'd begun to slump like a rag doll, hands dragging on the arena floor. The jacket had lost its shine. The oni didn't need Riku or the jacket any longer. They'd only been its tools. Now it was capable of growing and feeding on the crowd's energy all on its own.

The spins brought new applause from the audience and another foot of growth to the demon.

Step one. Step two. Step three. GO!

On the fourth beat, Song Yi swung the obsidian grid cloth out toward the oni while Willow and Iseul wrapped Riku in their plain black cloaks.

At that moment Ha Jun took the stage with a showstopping backflip. It was widely known that Ha Jun practiced martial arts: He'd done tricks onstage at smaller shows before. The fans loved it when he randomly popped on stage, so Ha Jun was able to keep up the illusion that he was part of a normal performance.

The audience loved Ha Jun extra, so the demon grew an inch in each leg.

Meanwhile, Ha Jun tackled Riku and held him down. It was easier than he'd imagined now that the man wasn't one with the demon. Riku fell to the ground on the fourth beat with a thunk that sounded like it was part of the song.

Song Yi knew her brother would be disappointed not to have a big fight onstage, but this was better. Ha Jun could hold Riku down while the demon was dispatched.

The obsidian cloak's grid rose into the air like an illusion to form a cage around the oni.

Iseul brought out the lantern trap.

ALIBI continued to circle the demon, dancing and spinning, while the bars of the cage tightened around its body, forcing the oni to get smaller and smaller. First it reverted to a normal horse size, then a goat, a rabbit, a hedgehog, and finally a mouse.

When they made it to the silly hair flip arc, Iseul grabbed the mouse and tossed it into the lantern.

Trapped at last, the demon howled for freedom.

The audience cheered wildly.

Riku thrashed suddenly with one last burst of power from a desperate demon, and Ha Jun flipped him over in an Olympic-worthy wrestling hold.

The girls tossed off their cloaks as if it were part of their dance, and the song came to an end.

"We did it!" Song Yi said, hugging her friends before the next track began. "Ha Jun will deliver the oni to a secret location where the producer will take him away." They were never told what happened once they delivered a demon, but ever since they'd become K-pop Demon Detectives, they'd never seen the same demon twice.

"We just need our jackets now," Willow said. "Then we can perform 'Red Pulse' at the end of the show and bring the Japan leg of our tour to a close with a *real* showstopper."

Ha Jun stood ready to escort Riku off the stage and take him to a place where they could question him after the concert.

Song Yi wasn't satisfied yet. She was determined to solve the last piece of the mystery. How had Riku gotten her jacket in the first place?

Minato said he'd only taken a selfie in it and then run off, leaving the jacket in the dressing room.

Next thing anyone knew, Riku was wearing the red jacket in the arena. And the demon was with him. The demon was too small at that point to drag the jacket off by itself. It must have gotten help. But from who?

After the show, they'd know everything.

The stage lights flickered for "Superstitious Wishes," their most mellow song. Willow had suggested using this song to calm the fans down after the takedown. Light sticks filled the darkness, creating a field of glowing shapes.

The plan now was for Ha Jun to slip offstage with Riku and, wearing gloves, remove the jacket from him. After confirming that the jacket was safe to wear, Yumi Kondo was there to make any necessary repairs and get the jacket ready for the final song and the big fashion reveal.

"Come on," Song Yi heard Ha Jun tell Riku. "Get up. It's over."

Riku suddenly popped to his feet and shouted, "It's not over until I say it's over!" He'd been mic'ed for the performance, and now suddenly the demon's voice echoed out of every speaker in the arena. Their song was interrupted. The fans looked around, confused.

Ha Jun took a karate stance, prepped to knock Riku down again. But before Ha Jun fully understood what was going on, Riku forced his way back onstage and, in a flash of movement, shoved Song Yi off the platform straight down into the first row of the audience. As the fans helped her get back up, Riku took Song Yi's place under the spotlight.

With a mighty show of physical strength, he grabbed the lapels of the red jacket and tore the coat in half. Sequins flew everywhere, rolling across the stage, shimmering and glistening under the spotlight.

And then Riku collapsed onto the stage.

Around him, every red sequin seemed to have a life inside of it. They popped up and down with a sizzling sound that filled the arena. The noise was chaotic and overwhelming. Fans covered their ears and raised their hoods to protect themselves from it.

"I will start anew!" the oni shrieked, its voice whipping through the area, disconnected now from Riku's limp body. "Watch me grow!"

CHAPTER 9

THE FINALE

“Don’t touch the sequins!” Song Yi shouted to her friends. They didn’t need reminding—they hurried over to pull Song Yi back onstage. It wasn’t a glamorous move, but they managed to get her up on the high platform without pulling her arms out.

“You okay?” Willow asked as Song Yi waved to the fans, assuring them she was fine.

Song Yi said softly, “Ego bruised, but otherwise okay. Never fallen off the stage before.”

“You were pushed,” Iseul reminded her.

“We gotta get back on track,” Willow said. “The videos from this concert are going to be online forever. We promised a great show, best show ever. How are we going to do that if the demon takes over?”

“The slow fish gets eaten last,” Song Yi said, recalling a saying from her brother’s martial arts master. The rest came clear. “The fish that swims ahead gets eaten first.” Her voice was confident. “If we bring all the sequins together, the oni will explode!”

“I still don’t understand, but I believe you,” Iseul said.

“It’s about the trapping of sudden fame, quick fortune,” Song Yi explained, glancing over at her brother in the wings. They locked eyes. “The oni is the fast fish, and that fish is about to find out why the rest of us take our time. Success isn’t easy; it takes hard work.”

“You sound like the master now,” Iseul said.

Song Yi laughed.

Willow said, “Let’s show this oni why you can’t steal someone else’s fans.”

“Uh, about the fans: I think they’re close to panicking. How are we going to make gathering the sequins look like a planned part of the show?” Iseul asked.

“If I knew that, I’d make my dive into the audience look planned, too,” Song Yi said.

“Oh, that one’s easy. I can add an audience crash to your dance moves at every show on the tour,” Willow suggested with a laugh. “It’ll be a meme!”

The next song on the revised list was “Wild Wild.” Then the video break. The fans were used to three tracks before the break.

Willow's eyes went wide. "I've got it." She looked at Song Yi. "It'll be a challenge. New dance steps, no rehearsal."

"You know I LOVE a challenge," Song Yi said with a grin. "Can I win?"

"We *all* win," Willow said, bringing them in for a huddle.

The opening notes for "Wild Wild" rang out, and Willow said, "Follow my lead."

Iseul and Song Yi nodded.

The trio formed a triangle, facing each other. When the first line rang out, "Wild, wild, wild child," they put their hands together in the center and focused on drawing the sequins forward with their energy.

Willow began to tap a pattern beat on the floor with her heel. The audience clapped along. "It's your four beats," Willow told Song Yi. "The fans will keep time for you."

"No counting?" Song Yi asked.

"You won't need to," Willow replied. The sequins were magically joining together and rolling slowly toward their triangle.

When the song sped up, Iseul took the lead vocals while Willow led them into a synchronized step back.

She swept her arm across her body, and then Iseul and Song Yi did the same. In unison, they all pressed their hands down.

Together, they rotated forward, then snapped back in with individual full-body spins.

The sequins pooled around them.

The demon's voice rang out, "You're bringing me back! Thank you, ALIBI!"

"Ignore it," Willow said. "We have to get the sequins all in one place. It's the only way."

"Wild, wild . . ." Song Yi took the vocals from Iseul as the sequins flattened into a compressed disk, then began to rise, like a sheet inhabited by a ghostly spirit.

Willow signaled another spin and a cross step. It was her turn for the vocals, but before she jumped in, she whispered, "Are any sequins missing?"

The sheet of sequins that had formed looked like there could be a person underneath the glowing red pattern, but as it rose off the stage, the shape stumbled forward.

"There's a sequin on the lift!" Iseul shouted, breaking off to dance her way to the center of the stage. She grabbed the sequin in her hand despite the burning sensation and tossed it toward the other sequins. It was immediately absorbed.

The blanket of red sequins attempted to rise again, but it didn't have the strength. It undulated up and down several times before falling back to the stage floor.

"Something's still wrong," Willow said, concern marking her brow. "This should be over."

"There is one more sequin!" Song Yi recalled. "I'll get it!" She improvised a dance move across to the side of the stage. That dance move would, unfortunately, later become a meme. "Ha Jun, quick. Where's my kimono?"

"Packed for Athens." He pulled it out of a nearby box.

She held out her hands, and he handed the robe to her. Song Yi awkwardly danced her way back across the stage.

"Last one's in my sleeve," she told the others.

"Fame and fortune are mine," the demon's voice echoed through the arena. "I am the most powerful oni on Earth!"

"Nah," said Song Yi. "You're just Tommy, a wee horned mouse oni that wants things handed to it the easy way."

"I've got the choreo," she assured Willow. To the oni, she said, "Watch and learn from an expert."

"One. Two. Three. Four!" Using a new series of terrible, awkward, out-of-rhythm steps, Song Yi turned the kimono inside out and dropped the final sequin into the pile with the others.

"I have it all!" the oni announced. "Fame . . . fortune . . . and—"

BOOM.

The gathering of sequins combusted into a tornado of swirling red smoke that swept across the stage. It was impossible to see through the dense crimson fog, but when the air cleared and the lights swept the stage, Willow, Iseul, and Song Yi stood together, hands raised, wearing their newly repaired Yumi Kondo designer jackets. They had succeeded, and were finally free to perform.

"Red Pulse" had been a popular song before that night.

After that night, it was legendary.

CHAPTER 10

THE FINAL CLUE

"Have you seen the internet?" Willow flashed her phone in Song Yi's face. "People are imitating your dance moves." She frowned. "Apparently, you're the group's new choreographer."

Song Yi leapt forward to hug Willow. "No one's replacing you."

"Millions of viewers love your moves!" Willow said. "I'm definitely adding the 'Song Yi Stumble' into our routine for Athens." She wiggled her hips. "And the 'Song Yi Shuffle.'" That was the move she'd invented to cross the stage for the kimono. "There's also the 'Song Yi Shake.'"

"I assume that's when I flung the sequin out of my kimono?" Song Yi leaned in to read the comments. "Ugh. To all this. I'm going to write a song called 'The Demon Made Me Do It.'"

"Our next big hit!" Willow cheered.

"Do we *all* have to fall off the stage?" Iseul asked while Ha Jun finished applying cream and wrapping her burned fingers.

"We can take turns pushing each other," Willow suggested with a chuckle.

"Ha Jun," said Song Yi, "Can you come up with something for the press to get us out of adding my steps to the routines?"

"My sister's ridiculous?" Ha Jun suggested.

"No, you are!" Song Yi countered.

Everyone laughed.

The group was backstage now, still in costume but resting on the luxury sofas. "Sorry about the Olympic stadium," Song Yi said. "But this is much nicer."

"No worries. We're going to Greece next," Ha Jun said, pressing the button to recline his chair. "Birthplace of the Olympics. Even though your new tutor will be coming along, I'm preparing a presentation." He closed his eyes. "I might need to ask the producer to buy me this chair."

"Demon-busting bonus?" Song Yi asked.

"I love this chair," he said with a long breath. During the show encore, Ha Jun had dropped Riku at home and brought the captured oni to the producer's secret location.

There was a small knock on the door. Song Yi batted her brother's feet. "No sleeping. We have an interview to conduct."

"We vanquished the demon," said Ha Jun. "Can't we rest? Do you have to know everything?"

"We need to know how Riku got the jacket," Song Yi said. She batted his feet again. "It's the manager's job to open the door."

"Really?" Ha Jun asked. "I didn't read that in my contract."

"I'll do it," Iseul jumped off her own couch and headed to the door. "I think I've solved that piece anyway."

"Lucky," Song Yi told Ha Jun as he settled back into his chair.

"Thanks, Iseul," he called out, shutting his eyes again.

"*Irasshaimase*, Yumi Kondo and Minato." Iseul gave the appropriate bow to their guests. "Please come in."

Yumi Kondo stepped back to let Minato enter first.

Song Yi raised her eyebrows at the act of deference. "Minato has been promoted," she said as they both sat. "And I gave him a raise."

"Yumi Kondo and I are going to see an American movie together tonight," Minato said, looking over at his employer. "I think we might be friends after all this."

The designer nodded. "You all made me understand things differently," Yumi Kondo said. "Thank you. In just a few hours, my life has changed. My website has never seen so much traffic!" She added, "I hope you'll accept the jackets as my gift for the rest of the tour."

"That's so nice!" Willow said. "We love them very much."

"I was hoping you would." Yumi Kondo told Song Yi, "Tonight, after the movie, I am going to seal the photonic silk residue with a new polymer. You won't have a dust problem ever again."

"Thank you," Song Yi said.

There was a short pause before Minato turned to Song Yi and asked, "You wanted to talk to us?" He glanced at the wall clock. "The movie starts in an hour."

"Minato," Song Yi began, "after you saw the demon here in the dressing room, you said you left the jacket behind to go and hide."

"I wasn't going to take an evil demon's jacket with me," he said. "Who would do that?!"

"That's what we want to know as well," Song Yi said. "Did you see anyone else come into the room between when you left the jacket here and when we arrived back to discover it was missing?"

"No. I was hiding." He sighed.

Song Yi smiled knowingly.

"Okay, have fun at the movies," Iseul said, standing.

"We don't have any more questions?" Ha Jun opened his eyes. "Maybe you want to know where Yumi Kondo was during that time? It was her pet demon, after all."

"Nah," Willow said. "Now we know who took it."

"Yes, we do," Song Yi said.

"Who?" Ha Jun asked. "Who took the jacket?"

"I thought you didn't want to know," Song Yi teased her brother.

"Now I do!" he said. "It's like the master said, 'Curiosity nibbles the cheese.'"

Willow and Iseul turned to Song Yi.

"Knowing comes when knowing needs," she quoted the master herself. "We'll find out what it means . . . someday." She turned to her brother. "Come with us, Cheese Nibbler, and we'll show you what we know."

In the hall, Yumi Kondo and Minato went one way as ALIBI and Ha Jun went the other.

In the center of the empty arena, there stood a raised platform. It was surrounded by metal barricades designed to keep fans out. Sound desks, lighting controls, video equipment, and computer stations filled a booth.

When the production was moved so quickly from Nippon Budokan to the Saitama Super Arena, there hadn't been time to call in all new staff. Those who had worked at the other arena just came along.

"Akiko," Iseul approached the booth. "Can we chat?"

"Of course!" Akiko stepped down from the platform. "How can I help you? Need to see more security footage? You should see how many cameras are in the halls here! No one goes anywhere without being watched."

"Good to know," Willow said, waving to the ceiling.

"Did you ever figure out what happened between 5:30 and 6:00 in the evening at Nippon Budokan?" Iseul asked.

Akiko tilted his head. "No. Was I supposed to? I thought we agreed it was a glitch."

"It wasn't a glitch," Iseul said. "I think it was a PoE switch overload triggered on purpose."

"A what?" Willow whispered in Song Yi's left ear.

"A what?" Ha Jun whispered in Song Yi's right ear.

She shrugged at them both.

"It has kept me up at night," Iseul said. "Why would the only camera in that hallway go to static for exactly the time we were away from the room?" She waited for Akiko to reply. In the silence, she said, "Because you plugged a high-draw device into the system while you snagged the jacket and hurried away."

"You have no proof," Akiko said.

"The dust," Iseul said. "I saw you blow dust off the computer keyboard, which might have seemed normal, except that we know Minato left the same kind of dust, photonic silk residue, behind when he had the jacket." Standing straight and confident, Iseul said, "You got the dust on the keyboard after you took the jacket."

"I . . ." Akiko didn't have another excuse. "It's true. I took the jacket."

"I know," Iseul said. "But what I can't figure out is why."

Song Yi wondered whether Akiko knew about the demon. If he did, it was unlikely he'd have stolen the jacket.

"I got a message on social from @LOVE-MY-ALIBI. He had a photo of the jacket already and offered me a lot of money to get it for him."

Willow sighed. "It's all because of Minato's selfie!"

"Minato truly didn't know," Song Yi said. "He took the photo and sent it. He didn't know the fan would want more."

"Why did Akiko turn off the camera when Minato first knocked on the door?" Song Yi asked. "That was *before* the selfie."

"Uh, I might have erased a little footage," Akiko told them, cringing. "I saw Minato come to the door and take the garment rack with him down the hall. And then I saw him come back." Akiko frowned. "I was ready to go investigate what was happening, but about a minute after Minato went into the dressing room, the social media message came."

"Ah yes. I see it more clearly now," Iseul said. She pulled out her notebook and reviewed what she'd written over the last few days. "You rushed to the room, grabbed Song Yi's costume, and stashed it in a place for Riku to pick up." She nodded, certain she was correct. "You had the dust on your fingers when you came back to the computer. It was on your keyboard from when you altered the footage."

"I suppose we're lucky you didn't try it on," Willow said. "That jacket would have given you delusions of fame and fortune like it did the others."

"I suppose that's a good thing," Akiko said. "But still, I took the jacket. I admit it, and I am sorry."

"I appreciate your honesty," Iseul said, logging out of the tablet and closing the cover. "Though you should have told us sooner."

"What do you want to do?" Ha Jun asked Iseul. "People can't just go around stealing designer costumes. We have to tell the authorities."

"Please," Akiko begged. "I have been the assistant for many, many years, and will never have the opportunity to become the director. If I don't find a way to make more money for my family . . ." Tears welled in his eyes. "I am desperate."

"Come work for us," Iseul immediately replied. "We can use someone to *manage* tech on the tour."

"What?!" Ha Jun shouted. He grabbed Iseul's arm, dragging her aside. "You can't just hire people at random. Especially not thieves!"

"Akiko is a good person," Willow said, placing a hand on her heart. "I feel it."

Iseul said, "And he knows a lot about show tech. But . . . I bet if we let him know about our side work, he'd be able to help me create *other* tech, too." She winked. It was a hint that the girls could use some upgraded gadgets for their side gigs.

Willow stood behind Iseul. "My instincts agree."

"I'm cool with it," Song Yi said. "It would be nice to build our own *trustworthy* team."

"What will the producer say?" Ha Jun asked. He knew he'd been bested. The girls weren't going to let him say no. "I suppose I'll find out." Ha Jun sighed, then stepped forward. "Come with me, Akiko, and we'll get the paperwork started. If you want, you'll join ALIBI in Athens."

Akiko restrained himself from leaping into Ha Jun's arms. "*Arigato gozaimasu.*" Akiko bowed. "*Arigato gozaimasu.*" He bowed once more. "*Arigato gozaimasu.*"

Once they were alone, Willow, Song Yi, and Iseul sat down in the stadium seats to go over the events of the day. They looked out at the stage where their final show had taken down a demon and where they'd won the hearts of thousands of new fans.

"We did it!" Willow said, taking a deep breath and feeling satisfied. "Case out the door, good vibes galore."

"Data checked, demon checked," Iseul giggled, kicking her feet up on the seats in front of her.

Song Yi pushed Iseul's boots down off the back of the chair and laughed. "How about this?" She hummed a few notes, then sang, “By the time we drop the final beat . . . the mystery’s solved, nice and neat!”

EPILOGUE

"Project AVF is a go!" Ha Jun told Willow, Iseul, and Song Yi. They'd traveled in the unmarked white van and were now at the curb outside the airport.

"I've already forgotten what that means," Song Yi told her brother as the driver slid open the door.

"Project Avoid Fans." Ha Jun rolled his eyes. "Do you ever listen to me?"

"Depends on what you're saying," Song Yi laughed. "How can we avoid fans when we're flying commercial? The producer has us sitting in the back of the plane where everyone will pass us on the way to the bathroom."

"That's not true," Ha Jun said. The girls gathered on the sidewalk. He handed them their tickets. "You're grouped together in a middle row. Only the people in front of you will pass by."

"Half the plane," Iseul said. "I suppose that is a little better."

"Where are you sitting?" Iseul asked Ha Jun.

"I'm a few rows ahead," he replied. "Managers need time off." Ha Jun held up his sleeping mask. "It's a twelve-hour flight." He yawned. "Twelve whole hours without my sister and her friends nagging at me!" He imitated them. "Ha Jun, find Yumi Kondo. Ha Jun, hire my nerdy new friend. Ha Jun, make sure I have a vegetarian meal." He clasped his hands together and whined, "Ha Jun, save us from the demon."

"That last one isn't true," Iseul said through her laughter. "The others are right-on, though. And that's a pretty decent imitation of Willow!"

"The master says, 'Carrot. Cow. Taco,'" Willow replied in her best Ha Jun voice. "The master is so wise . . ."

Song Yi and Iseul laughed until they both cried.

"And this is *exactly* why I am sitting by myself," Ha Jun said, grabbing his own suitcase and the jackets, now in one garment bag. He walked into the airport alone.

"Wait for us!" Song Yi called after him.

Willow, Song Yi, and Iseul were all wearing comfy clothing for the long flight. Song Yi had on an oversized black jacket with a ruby sports tank and black joggers. Iseul was wearing a thrifted gray T-shirt and sweatpants with old farm-worn boots. Willow had on her new fancy tennis shoes, pairing them with a light blue sweatshirt and a long cargo skirt.

The fans weren't waiting outside the airport, but once ALIBI stepped up to the gate, they immediately mobbed them.

"Project AVF fail!" Song Yi called to her brother as a hundred cameras flashed in her face.

"Not for me," Ha Jun said. No one at the airport wanted to take his photo, so for him Project AVF was a success. "See you in Greece."

Ha Jun was gone.

ALIBI hadn't had this much attention at an airport before, but last night's show for 40,000 fans equaled millions of hits online. Just as Song Yi expected, the fans thought the demon's growth and subsequent vanquishment were part of the show. She hoped the audience in Greece didn't expect the same finale. It was a "you had to be there" experience.

For Willow, Song Yi, and Iseul, it would be a long slog to the gate flanked by security guards and blinded by camera flashes.

"Song Yi!"

She heard someone call her name, but ignored it, assuming it was paparazzi.

"Willow!"

Willow also ignored the call.

"Iseul! Iseul! I need your input on this scrub."

That got Iseul's attention. Iseul turned. "Wow! Akiko!" She rushed toward a row of screaming fans.

ALIBI's newest employee gave Iseul a hug, while Song Yi and Willow posed for the cameras. It seemed the right thing to do while they waited. Besides, people might stop screaming at them if they gave them some good photos to post.

It turned out, according to Akiko, that instead of going straight to Athens to get ready, ALIBI was heading to a secret seaside rehearsal space for a few days. Akiko would meet them there.

The plan change was exciting. Willow wanted to work out a few new dance steps for the Athens concert. Song Yi was working on a new song. She'd bought a cute blank book back at the mall for her poetry and lyrics. It had Japanese cherry blossoms on the cover. And Iseul had been working on techy ideas and schematics to share with Akiko.

It was only a few days' break, but they couldn't wait. So much to do!

Akiko gave Iseul another hug and handed her a messenger bag. She held the bag to her chest as she returned.

"What's that?" Song Yi asked, eyeing the leather satchel. There was a fancy technical lock holding the bag shut.

"Gifts," she told Song Yi and Willow. "I had a few ideas and Akiko made prototypes." She grinned. "Fingers crossed no one stops me at security!"

At the metal detectors, a scanner picked up something in the bag, but after getting a series of personalized ALIBI videos for his daughter and her friends, the agent "forgot" all about it.

The girls hurried to the gate just as the flight boarded.

Hordes of fans, many from other flights at other gates, blocked the way.

The announcers called, "All rows have now boarded."

"We aren't going to make it," Iseul said, looking at the crowd between themselves and the gate.

"I'll call Ha Jun," Song Yi said, pulling out her phone.

"No need," he shouted from the gate. "I'm here." Ha Jun rushed to his team and began threatening karate moves at the crowd.

"Can't miss the flight," he told the fans, swinging his hands in a gentle knifehand strike. "You want to see ALIBI online . . . gotta let them through. Don't make me hurt you!" He added, "Check out my videos on my social and be sure to follow me. You'll see what I can do!" He swept his hands, slicing the air.

Ha Jun's threats were effective; most everyone around them had seen him take down Riku, and though it wasn't as dramatic as it appeared online, they quickly moved aside.

To give the fans a little tease before ALIBI got on board, Ha Jun winked and called out, "We have more surprises . . . watch for them!"

"Welcome aboard," the gate agent greeted them.

Once on the plane, Song Yi was between Iseul and Willow. She tried to ask about the messenger bag, but Iseul said it had to wait until they got to Greece. In the meantime, Iseul wouldn't let the bag out of her sight, wrapping a long copper cord around the handle and attaching it firmly to her wrist before putting on headphones. Iseul took off her glasses, set her head against the window, and closed her eyes.

Song Yi couldn't sleep. The Tokyo concert had been exciting and the adrenaline from almost missing the flight coursed through her.

Up ahead, her brother could be heard talking to his seatmates. She decided to chance a few photos and go see what was up.

"Can I climb over?" she asked. While Iseul snoozed, Willow was reading *Ghosts of Greece*.

"Where did you get that book?" Song Yi asked as Willow tucked in her knees to let her pass.

"I picked it up at the mall," Willow said. "When I bought the obsidian cloak and lantern that we needed to catch the demon." She shrugged. "Impulse buy."

"Your impulses are usually right-on," Song Yi said.

"Hope not," Willow replied. "If you thought Japanese demons were hard to vanquish, Greek ones are even more difficult."

"ALIBI will always reveal the truth," Song Yi said, steadying herself in the aisle.

Ha Jun was sitting on the aisle about five rows forward. Song Yi let the cameras around her flash, even posing for a young girl before reaching her brother.

"Are you in Premium Economy?" she asked, seeing that he had more legroom than the rest of them.

"The producer wanted extra space for our guests," Ha Jun said.

It was then that Song Yi realized Ha Jun wasn't just chatting with strangers. He knew his seatmates!

"Song Yi," Ha Jun said, "this is Kyria Melina." He whispered, "That's Greek for Mrs. Melina." Then louder, "And her daughter, Elara."

Elara looked to be fifteen years old, just shy of Ha Jun's age. She had round, dark eyes and strawberry hair like her mom. Kyria Melina wore her curls in a tight, severe bun. Elara let hers flow naturally down to her shoulders, unbrushed and wild.

"Can I get a photo?" she asked. "I'm your *biggest* fan."

"I think we already met our biggest fan," Song Yi said with a laugh. "Maybe you don't want to be *that*."

Elara looked confused.

"Never mind my sister," Ha Jun said. "While we are in Greece, the two of you will become great friends."

"We will?" Song Yi asked.

"Kyria Melina will be your school tutor while we are in Greece," Ha Jun said. "And Elara will be doing schoolwork with you, Iseul, and Willow."

"Exciting!" Elara cheered, taking several candid photos of Song Yi's wide-eyed face. "Ha Jun promised you'd teach me to dance, too!" She rubbed her hands together. "When can we start?!"

"Surprise!" Ha Jun said with a grin.

"You do love to shock us, don't you?" Song Yi said with a nod. While she might have thought their tutor, as assigned by the producer, would be from Korea, it was nice that they'd get to learn Greek history from a pro. Elara might be a handful, but between the break and the concerts, they'd only be in Greece a week.

ALIBI could handle anything for seven days.

"Any other surprises?" Song Yi asked her brother.

"Knowing comes when knowing needs." He grinned.

"*I* know something." Elara rose up in her middle seat, leaned in way too close for comfort, and whispered to Song Yi, "The seaside amphitheater that we're staying at is haunted." With a chuckle, she pulled back and gave Song Yi an exaggerated wink. "I love a ghost story, don't you?"

DISCOVER MORE K-POP DEMON DETECTIVES

BOOK 2

GHOSTED IN GREECE

BOOK 3

RIVALS IN ROME

BOOK 4

CALIFORNIA CURSE

BOOK 5

BANGKOK BETRAYAL

BOOK 6

ISTANBUL INTRIGUE